THE WORLD OF NORM

MAY CONTAIN BUTS

ORCHARD BOOKS
First published in Great Britain in 2015 by Orchard Books
First published in Great Britain in 2016 by The Watts Publishing Group

3 5 7 9 10 8 6 4 2

Text © Jonathan Meres 2015
Illustrations © Donough O'Malley 2015

The moral rights of the author and illustrator have been asserted.

A CIP catalogue record for this book
is available from the British Library.

ISBN 978 1 40835 542 8

Printed and bound in Great Britain by CPI Group (UK) Ltd, Croydon, CR0 4YY

The paper and board used in this book are from well-managed forests
and other responsible sources.

MIX
Paper from
responsible sources
FSC® C104740
FSC
www.fsc.org

Orchard Books
An imprint of
Hachette Children's Group
Part of The Watts Publishing Group Limited
Carmelite House
50 Victoria Embankment
London EC4Y 0DZ

An Hachette UK Company
www.hachette.co.uk

www.hachettechildrens.co.uk

JONATHAN MERES

THE WORLD OF NORM

NORM

MAY CONTAIN BUTS

ORCHARD

To anyone who's ever wanted a book
dedicated to them. This is for you.

CHAPTER 1

Norm knew it was going to be one of those days when he went to the toilet, just for something to do. It wasn't as if he **needed** to go to the toilet. It wasn't all that long since he'd actually **been**. And as far as Norm was aware he didn't have an abnormally small bladder. Not that Norm had ever spent much time thinking about the capacity of his bladder. Or **any** time thinking about the capacity of his bladder, for that matter. And it wasn't as if he particularly **liked** going to the toilet, either. It was all right. Nothing special. It was just another one of those things you had to do, along with breathing, sleeping and, in Norm's case, stuffing his face with as much margherita pizza as he could get his hands on.

The problem was, Norm was bored. Not just the **usual** kind of bored. Bored like he'd never been bored before. And when it came to being bored, Norm was something of an expert. But this boredom was somehow different. This boredom felt like it was taking boredom to a whole new level. If being bored had been an Xbox game, Norm would have already won. Now he was so bored he thought relieving **himself** might actually **relieve** his boredom. Even then, he wasn't **entirely** convinced. But it was worth a shot. He had to do **something** to pass the time before he went biking with his best friend Mikey. What else was he supposed to do? Tidy his flipping **room**? Right, thought Norm. Like **that** was ever going to happen!

"Is that you in there, Norman?" said a muffled voice from the other side of the bathroom door – though not quite so muffled that Norm didn't immediately know who it was.

"Go away, Dave!"

"I'll take that as a yes, then."

"Take it however you flipping want, you little freak!" spat Norm.

"Language," said Dave.

Norm sighed. This kind of situation would never happen if they had two flipping toilets like they used to. Or if his mum and dad had stopped after just one child. Either way it was **so** flipping annoying.

"What are you **doing** in there?"

"What do you **think** I'm doing, Dave, you doughnut?"

"One of two things," said Dave.

"So have a wild guess, then," said Norm. "You've got a fifty-fifty chance of getting it right."

"Having a pee?"

"Wrong," said Norm.

"Aw, yuk!" said Dave.

"What do you mean, yuk?" said Norm. "It's perfectly **natural!**"

"**Yours** aren't natural!"

Norm couldn't help smiling. Dave frequently drove him up the flipping wall, just like his other brother did. But unlike Brian, Dave could occasionally be quite funny, too.

"Have you finished yet?" said Dave.

"No I **haven't** flipping finished yet!" said Norm. "Clear off!"

"No," said Dave.

"What do you mean, no?"
said Norm.

"I need a pee!"

"Well, tough," said Norm.
"You'll just have to flipping wait,
won't you?"

"I can't," said Dave. "I'm going to
wet myself."

"Good."

"*That's* not very nice."

"So?" said Norm.

"So how long are you going to be?"

"Gordon flipping Bennet!" said Norm beginning
to get more and more frustrated. "I don't flipping
know how long I'm going to be! A flipping long time
if you don't flipping shut up and leave me to it!"

"Right, I'm telling," said Dave.

"Telling **what**?" said Norm.

But there was no reply. Dave was already halfway down the stairs.

Norm thought for a moment. He'd only gone to the toilet for something to do. But now he was there, he might as well do it.

CHAPTER 2

Norm wasn't particularly surprised to find his **brothers** sitting at the kitchen table when he eventually came downstairs. He did **live** with them after all. Un-flipping-fortunately. But there was nothing much he could **do** about it. Not for a good while yet, anyway, what with him still only being twelve years old. Or, as Norm preferred to think of it, nearly thirteen. He was, however, genuinely surprised to find Grandpa sitting **with** his brothers.

Pleasantly surprised, but surprised all the same.

"Hi, Grandpa. Didn't know you were coming."

"Neither did I," said Grandpa.

Norm pulled a face. Surely Grandpa must have known he was coming at **some** point. He hadn't just magically **appeared**, like in some stupid book.

"I just thought, well, it's Saturday morning. Why not visit my favourite grandchildren?"

"Ah, that's nice, Grandpa," said Brian.

Grandpa nodded. "Yes, but they weren't in, so I came here instead."

Dave burst out laughing straightaway. "Good one, Grandpa!"

"What?" said Brian. "Oh right. I get it. Yeah, good one, Grandpa!"

Norm sighed.

"What's up with *you*, Cheerful Charlie?" said Grandpa.

"What?" said Norm distractedly. "Oh, nothing. I'm just bored, that's all."

Grandpa scrutinised Norm for a moment, his cloud-like eyebrows almost meeting in the middle.

"Bored?"

Norm nodded.

"*Bored?*" repeated Grandpa, sounding slightly incredulous.

"Yeah," said Norm.

"How can you be **bored?**"

Norm shrugged. "Easy."

"Kids today."

Norm waited for Grandpa to go on. And on. And on. Probably with some boring story about people in the olden days **never** being bored because they were too busy making their own flipping entertainment, or whatever. But he didn't.

"What about them, Grandpa?"
said Norm.

"What about **what?**" said
Grandpa.

"Kids today?"

Grandpa screwed up his face
in concentration.

"It'll come to me in a minute."

Norm laughed. It was difficult not to sometimes with Grandpa.

"So what's the word on the street, Norman?"

Norm shrugged again. "Don't ask **me**."

"Give way," said Brian.

"What?" said Norm.

"Give way," said Brian. "**That's** the word on the street. In big white letters."

"Uh?" said Norm.

"Just before you get to the main road," said Brian. "You must have seen it, Norman."

"That's two words," said Dave.

"What?" said Brian.

"Give way is actually *two* words."

"Yeah? So?" said Brian defensively.

"So...you stink, Brian!" said Dave.

"Oh yeah?" said Brian.

"Yeah," said Dave.

"Well, you...you...you..."

"What?" said Dave.

"Just wait," said Brian.

"Gordon flipping Bennet," muttered Norm. "Is that the best you can do, Brian?"

"Ooh, that reminds me, Norman," said Dave.

"What does?" said Norm.

"Me saying that Brian stinks."

"Uh? What are you on about?"

"I hope you remembered to open the bathroom window."

"Shut **up**, Dave!"

"Ah, so you've been dropping the kids off, have you, Norman?" said Grandpa.

"What?" said Norm.

"Dropping the kids off at the pool?"

Norm pulled a face. "Uh?"

"It means having a poo," said Dave. "Think about it."

Norm thought about it.

"It's a euphemism," added Brian helpfully.

"A **what**-amism?" said Norm.

"A euphemism," said Brian. "When you say something instead of saying something **else**."

"What's the point of **that**?" said Norm. "Why not just say what you **want** to say? It's much easier."

"Yes but it might not always be **polite**," said Dave.

"Right," said Norm, who was beginning to have less and less of a clue what anybody was talking about, let alone what a flipping **euphemism** was. Would it make any difference if he left the room and came back in again, he wondered? Probably not.

"Hello, Dad. Didn't know you were coming," said

Norm's mum appearing in the doorway, a bulging carrier bag in each hand.

"Oh, you know me," said Grandpa.

Everybody looked at Grandpa, waiting for him to continue. But once again he didn't.

"What are you doing, love?" said Norm's mum, turning to Norm.

"Who, me?" said Norm.

Norm's mum nodded.

"Right now?"

"Right now," said Norm's mum.

"Nothing much," said Norm. Which was true. He wasn't doing much. Actually he wasn't doing **anything**. But Norm knew immediately that he'd just made a big mistake.

"Good," said Norm's mum, plonking down the carrier bags on a worktop and starting to unpack. "In that case you can do the recycling."

Norm looked at his mum as if she'd just told him to build a new conservatory. Not that they had an **old** conservatory. Or **any** conservatory, for that matter.

"Seriously?"

Norm's mum stopped what she was doing and turned around.

"Why would I joke about doing the recycling?"

It was a fair point, thought Norm. Why **would** she? His mum wasn't exactly renowned for her blistering one-liners. If she **said** something she generally **meant** it.

"You said you were **bored**, Norman," said Brian. "It'll be something to do!"

"Shut **up**, Brian you little freak," hissed Norm under his breath.

"Did you?" said Norm's mum.

"Did I what?"

"Say you were bored?"

"Might've done."

"You **might** have done?"

"He did, Mum!" said Dave. "I heard him!"

Norm sighed. "OK, OK. I did."

"Excellent," said Norm's mum. "Off you go, then."

"What?" said Norm showing no sign of making a move.

"What are you waiting for?"

What was he **waiting** for? thought Norm. Where did he flipping **start?**

"Well?"

"But..."

"No buts, love. You're doing the recycling and that's all there is to it."

"Why can't **they** do it?" said Norm, glaring venomously at his brothers.

"Why can't they do **what?**" said Norm's dad appearing in the doorway, also carrying a couple of carrier bags.

"Nothing," said Norm quickly.

Nom's dad pulled a face.

"Why can't they do **nothing**?"

"The recycling," said Dave.

"Oh, I see," said Norm's dad.

"We **could** do it," said Brian. "Couldn't we, Dave?"

Dave nodded. "No probs."

Flipping **creeps**, thought Norm.

"Actually you **couldn't** do it," said Norm's dad.

"Couldn't we?" said Brian.

"Aw, why not, Dad?" said Dave sounding quite disappointed.

Norm's dad hesitated for a couple of seconds before breaking into a smile.

"Because I thought we could go swimming instead."

"YEAAAAH! SWIMMING!" sang Brian and Dave together.

"Any chance of a lift home?" said Grandpa.

"Absolutely," said Norm's dad. "Once I've dropped the kids off at the pool."

There was a moment's silence before Norm eventually piped up.

"Dad?"

"Yes, Norman?"

"Is that a eupha-thingy?"

Norm's dad looked puzzled. "A eupha-thingy?"

"He means a **euphemism**," said Brian.

"Oh right, no," said Norm's dad.

"So you're actually dropping them off at the pool?"

"Yes, of course I am. Why?"

"Just wondered," said Norm heading for the door.

CHAPTER 3

Norm stood in the entrance to the garage and let his eyes adjust to the gloom. Gradually he began to make out the shapes of the various recycling bins, but only **after** he'd made out the shape of his precious mountain bike first. Why couldn't Mikey go biking **now**? Why did they have to wait till the flipping afternoon? **Anything** could happen before **then**! It was **so** unfair.

Norm sighed. He really couldn't see the point of recycling. Then again, there were a lot of things Norm couldn't see the point of. His two little brothers, for instance. What exactly was the point of **them**? Apart from constantly irritating him and winding him up and generally getting on his flipping nerves? Because apart from **that** they seemed to serve no purpose whatso- flipping- ever.

It was the same when it came to sorting out the rubbish. Who actually **cared** if you chucked a flipping jam jar into one particular coloured bin or a flipping Coco Pops packet into another? How exactly was **that** supposed to save the flipping planet? That was just staggeringly **stupid**, as far as Norm was concerned. Why not just bung it in the **same** bin? It would save an awful lot of bottoming about. And an awful lot of time, too. Time which could be far better spent...well, mountain biking, for a flipping start!

No, what was **much** more important, as far as **Norm** was concerned, was the fact that the Coco Pops packets they were chucking out these days were all flipping supermarket own brand Coco Pops packets. Not like back in the day, when they could afford **proper** flipping Coco Pops. And a proper flipping **house** to eat 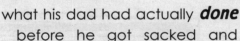 them in, too. When his dad actually had a **job**. Not that Norm ever knew what his dad had actually **done** before he got sacked and they'd had to move and Norm had woken up and found himself about to pee in a wardrobe. When life was – well, if not actually **sweet**, at least considerably **sweeter** than it was now.

Norm took a deep breath and exhaled noisily. A little **too** noisily, as it turned out.

"Is that you in there, **Norman?**" said a voice. A voice which Norm knew only too well. A voice which never **ever** failed to drive him abso-flipping-lutely **bananas**.

"Who's that?"

"Ha, ha. Very funny," said Chelsea.

Norm stopped what he was doing – not that he'd actually started doing anything yet – and stepped out of the shadows, shielding his eyes from the glare of the sun.

"Oh, it's you."

"What's the matter, **Norman?**" Chelsea grinned. "Dazzled by my aura?"

"Can I ask you a question?" said Norm, deliberately ignoring Chelsea's question. Not that he knew what an aura was, anyway.

"I don't know, **Norman**. Can you?"

"Why do you always say my name like that?"

"Like what, **Norman?**" said Chelsea, if anything overemphasising Norm's name even **more** than she usually did.

"Like **that**," said Norm trying not to get **too** annoyed even though it was already way too late for that.

Chelsea smiled. "Because it's funny."

"You reckon?"

"Yes, I **do**, actually."

"Well, it's...it's..."

"**What** is it, **Norman?**" said Chelsea.

Flipping annoying, thought Norm. **That's** what it was. What right did **she** have to say whether someone's name was flipping funny or not? Who did she think she was? The flipping Minister of Names, or something? Thank **goodness** she only lived next door with her dad at weekends and that he only had to put up with it for two days a week. And that was **another** thing. Why did Chelsea **always** have to pop up on the other side of the flipping fence, whenever he was outside? She was like a spider, lying in wait for a fly to land on her web.

"Well?" said Chelsea. "***What*** is it?"

Norm sighed. What was the point? Nothing he said now was ever going to make any difference. Not that he'd actually ***thought*** of anything to say yet. He could be here till the flipping cows came home and he probably ***still*** wouldn't think of anything. It was so annoying.

"I'll tell you what it is," said Chelsea. "It's an old man's name."

Norm pulled a face. "No, it's not."

"Yes, it is."

Norm sighed again.

"Listen to you," said Chelsea. "You even ***sound*** like

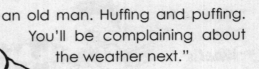

an old man. Huffing and puffing. You'll be complaining about the weather next."

"Uh?" said Norm. "No, I won't. What's wrong with the weather?"

"Nothing," said Chelsea. "But that's what old people do. They complain about nothing."

Norm thought for a moment. He wasn't quite sure how it was possible to complain about **nothing**, but right now he was more concerned with getting one over on Chelsea.

"Well, at least..."

"At least what, **Norman?**" said Chelsea cutting him off. "At least you're not named after a football team? Because I've never heard **that** one before!"

Norm hated it when other people were sarcastic. It was OK for **him** to be sarcastic. That was different.

But other people? That just wasn't on.

"I wasn't going to say that," said Norm, even though that was **_precisely_** what he was going to say.

"Really?" said Chelsea.

"Really," said Norm.

"What were you going to say, then, **_Norman?_**"

"Erm..."

"Exactly!" said Chelsea triumphantly.

"Hi di hi," said Grandpa emerging from the front door, Brian and Dave buzzing about him like flies on a fresh cowpat.

"Hi, Chelsea!" shrieked Brian.

"Hi!" said Chelsea. "Did you remember to wash your hands, Dave?"

Brian looked puzzled. "How do you know Dave needs to wash his hands?"

"Our little secret," said Chelsea. "Isn't that right, Dave?"

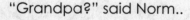

Dave shrugged innocently. "Dunno what you're talking about."

"Grandpa?" said Norm..

"Yes, Norman?"

"Chelsea reckons old people complain about **nothing**."

"Oh, **does** she now?" said Grandpa.

"No offence." Chelsea grinned.

Grandpa looked at Chelsea. "Why would *I* be offended by that?"

"Erm..."

"Do you think I'm *old*, or something?"

"Erm..." said Chelsea again.

Norm chuckled quietly. All of a sudden Chelsea seemed slightly flustered and not quite so full of herself as usual. It was **brilliant**.

"What do you call *old*?" said Grandpa.

Chelsea thought for a moment. "Over thirty?"

"Over **thirty?**" said Grandpa. "In that case it's a wonder I'm still *alive*."

"**You're** not old, Grandpa!" said Dave. "You're... you're..."

"What?" said Grandpa.

"Annually challenged?" said Brian hopefully.

Grandpa's eyes crinkled ever so slightly in the corners. It was the closest he ever came to smiling. "How old are **you** now, Brian?"

"Ten," said Brian.

"Really?" said Grandpa. "That's a coincidence."

Brian looked puzzled. "Why?"

"I was ten when I was your age."

Dave burst out laughing straightaway. "Good one, Grandpa!"

"What?" said Brian. "Oh, right. I geddit. Yeah, good one, Grandpa!"

"Grandpa?" said Dave.

"What is it?"

"I'm seven."

"What do you want, Dave?" said Norm. "A flipping medal?"

"Language," said Dave.

"Shut up," said Norm.

"Right, come on, you lot!" said Norm's dad appearing in the doorway and heading towards the car. "In you get."

"Bye, Chelsea!" shrieked Brian, rushing headlong down the drive.

"Bye, guys!" called Chelsea waving frantically.

"Toodle pip," said Grandpa ambling slowly after the others.

"Yeah, see you later, Grandpa," said Norm.

"Hopefully."

"What do you mean, *hopefully*?" said Norm.

"If I've not kicked the bucket by then," said Grandpa without turning around.

"Your grandpa's well funny," said Chelsea.

"Yeah," said Norm. "He is."

"Where are they going?"

"Swimming."

"Swimming?" said Chelsea.

"Well, Grandpa's not. But the others are."

"Why aren't *you* going, **Norman?**"

Why wasn't he going swimming? thought Norm as the car drove off. Gordon flipping Bennet! What kind of stupid question was that? Firstly he was supposed to be going biking with Mikey. Not that Chelsea could be expected to know *that* of course. Secondly he'd rather go to **IKEA** than go swimming. And he'd rather set fire to his flipping **teeth** than go to IKEA. Actually, thought Norm, that wasn't strictly true. It wasn't so much the thought of going **swimming**. It was the thought of going swimming with his noisy, smelly little brothers, in a place which frankly, was noisy and smelly enough already.

"Well?" said Chelsea.

"It's like a flipping toilet," said Norm.

"What is?"

"The swimming pool."

"It's not **that** bad!" said Chelsea.

"Flipping is," said Norm. "It's a waste of time **having** toilets in swimming pools. Swimming pools basically **are** toilets!"

Chelsea laughed.

"I'm serious!" said Norm. "Why

do you think the water's always warmer when you swim past a baby?"

"You know something, **Norman?**"

"What?"

"You're quite funny too."

"What?"

"You heard."

Chelsea was right. Norm **had** heard. He just wasn't sure how to react. On the one hand he couldn't give a flying monkey's whether Chelsea thought he was funny or not. Her opinions were of no interest to him.

40

None whatso-flipping-ever. On the other hand...
Norm thought for a moment. Actually there **wasn't**
another hand. He couldn't care **less** what Chelsea
thought. Or so he thought.

"I'll miss you."

"What?" said Norm.

"I said I'll miss you," said Chelsea.

Norm pulled a face. "What do you mean?"

Chelsea shrugged. "I mean I'll **miss** you."

Norm was confused. He knew what the words
meant. What he **didn't** understand was why
Chelsea had actually **said** them.

"When I **move**," said Chelsea.

Norm gawped like a goldfish for several seconds.
Again, he knew what Chelsea had actually **said**.
But the word **move** could mean several things. He
didn't **dare** believe – or **hope** – that she meant
what he **thought** she meant.

"Don't tell me you haven't noticed, **Norman**!" Chelsea laughed.

"Noticed what?" said Norm.

"I don't believe it."

"DON'T BELIEVE WHAT?"

yelled Norm unable to contain his frustration a moment longer.

"Look," said Chelsea pointing towards the street.

Norm swivelled round and looked. There at the end of the drive, on Chelsea's side of the fence, was a sign stuck into the ground. A sign with two words on it.

Norm stared in disbelief. As far as he could see there were two possibilities. Either a) he was dreaming, or b) this was some kind of massive wind-up. If the

answer was a)
he was going
to be gutted when he
eventually woke up. And if
it was b) he sincerely hoped
no one was filming it on their
phone so that they could post it
on YouTube or send it to one of those
TV programmes that showed clips of people falling
off trampolines and old men's trousers falling down
at weddings. One thing was for sure. This couldn't
possibly *really* be happening? Could it?

"Well?" said Chelsea. "Aren't you going to say something?"

Even if Norm **had** been able to think of something to say, he couldn't have actually **said** it. He'd temporarily lost the power of speech.

"How are you getting on, love?" said Norm's mum from the front door. "Oh, hello, Chelsea. Didn't see you there."

"Hi!" said Chelsea.

"I see you're moving."

Chelsea nodded. "Yeah."

Whoa, thought Norm. It was beginning to look like this really **was** happening!

"Be sorry to see you go."

Norm looked at his mum. Sorry? To see Chelsea **go?** Was she out of her mind? This was the best news since...since...since. Well, since **ever**, basically.

"I'll be sorry, too," said Chelsea. "Well, I mean I've only ever been here at weekends. But even so..."

Even *so*, thought Norm. This was *still* the best flipping news, *ever*! It was like all Christmases and birthdays rolled into one. Right now, Norm quite literally could not be any happier.

"So?" said Norm's mum turning her attention back to Norm.

"So, what?" croaked Norm.

"How are you getting on?"

"With what?"

"The recycling?"

"Oh, right," said Norm. "That."

"Yes, *that*," said Norm's mum.

"Erm. Haven't actually started yet, Mum."

"Well, in that case you'd better get cracking, then, hadn't you?"

"'Kay," said Norm, heading back into the garage.

Norm's mum smiled at Chelsea. "What is he *like*?"

"How long have you got?" Chelsea grinned.

CHAPTER 4

Norm was still in a slight state of shock as he started sifting through the rubbish and chucking it into the appropriate coloured plastic containers. So at least he'd have a good excuse if he got anything wrong. Not that Norm was in the least bit bothered if he *did* get anything wrong. He was *way* too happy. Nothing was going to dampen his mood. Not even doing the stupid recycling.

Of course Norm knew that it wouldn't last. He knew that as sure as night followed day, *bad* things were bound to follow *good* things. At least in *Norm's* experience they flipping were, anyway. Not that all that many *good* things ever happened to

night→day
good things → bad things

Norm in the first place, of course. But when they did, something else usually happened pretty much immediately afterwards to bring him crashing straight back down to earth again. And usually with a bang. Right now, though, Norm simply couldn't *imagine* what that something could possibly be.

A worldwide pizza dough shortage? Nah. News of an imminent alien invasion? Whatever. Chelsea was moving house! He was *finally* going to see the back of her. He'd never have to worry about her popping up on the other side of the fence and saying his name in that really annoying way, *ever* again! Compared to *that*, a pizza dough shortage and an alien invasion seemed completely unimportant!

Yes, it was true that Chelsea only actually lived next door with her dad at *weekends* – and that she spent the rest of the week at her mum's – but that made no difference as far as Norm was concerned. She was still, without any doubt whatso-flipping-ever, one of **the** most irritating people he'd ever had the misfortune to know. Not that Norm really **knew** Chelsea all that well. And now, thanks to that 'For Sale' sign at the end of the drive, he never flipping **would**.

Norm's phone rang.

"Hello?" he said, whipping it out of his pocket and answering.

"Hi," said Mikey on the other end of the line.

"Oh hi, Mikey!"

"Didn't you know it was me, Norm?"

"Course I knew it was you, you doughnut!" Norm laughed. "You're about the only person who ever flipping **calls!** Well, apart from my parents. But they don't count."

"You sound like you're in a good mood," said Mikey.

"Yeah, well, that's because I **am** in a good mood actually. As a matter of fact I'm in a **very** good mood!"

"Why's that, then?" said Mikey.

Norm turned to look outside. His mum and Chelsea had both disappeared. But he lowered his voice just in case there was a chance of being overheard.

"I'll tell you later, Mikey, all right? What time you coming over?"

"Ah, well that's the thing."

Norm pulled a face. "What's the thing?"

"I can't come over."

"What do you mean?" said Norm. "Why not?"

"My brakes need fixing."

"Your brakes?"

"Yeah."

"Bummer," said Norm.

"**Big** bummer," said Mikey.

Norm laughed.

"What's so funny?" said Mikey.

"You said 'big bummer'."

There was a sigh on the other end of the line. "Are you coming over, or what, Norm?"

"What?" said Norm.

"Well, if I can't come over to **your** place, you'd better come over to **mine**."

Norm thought for a moment. "Fair enough."

"Good," said Mikey.

"I'll be over after lunch," said Norm.

"'Kay," said Mikey.

"See you then," said Norm.

"See you then," said Mikey.

There you go, thought Norm to himself, pressing a key and ending the call. A perfect example of a **bad** thing immediately following a **good** thing. Except that on this occasion, the **good** thing was just so unbe-flipping-lievably good, nothing could possibly bring him crashing back down to earth again. Abso-flipping-lutely **nothing**.

CHAPTER 5

Norm bolted down the slice of supermarket own brand pizza as quickly as possible, gulped down a glass of own brand cola, burped a couple of own brand burps – and got straight on his bike.

It didn't take long to get to Mikey's house. Although that very much depended on which way Norm chose to go. If he went via Indonesia, for instance, it would probably take ages. But if Norm took a slightly more direct route to Mikey's, it didn't take long at all. Back when he lived just round the corner from his best friend it might only take one song on his iPod. Sometimes – depending on the length of the song – not even that. These days, though, it could easily take as long as four or five songs. Especially if Norm went via the woods behind the shopping precinct. And if he went via the woods – as he just had – then he might as well go **through** the precinct so that he could jump the set of steps. As he was just **about** to...

WORLD MOUNTAIN BIKE CHAMPION for the 10th year in a row

Norm pedalled as fast as he could and launched himself into the air. He might have only actually been **in** the air for the very briefest of moments – but even so it was long enough to imagine himself standing on the winner's podium, having just been crowned World Mountain Biking Champion for the tenth year in a row.

Although frankly, thought Norm, he'd probably settle for **one** year in a row.

"Oi! Watch where you're going!" someone yelled as Norm executed a perfect landing, before zooming off again.

Not that Norm **heard** of course, what with listening to his iPod. And even if he **had** heard he wouldn't have **cared**. Mainly because he was still **ecstatic** as a result of just finding out that Chelsea would soon be history. But also because Norm was never, **ever** happier than when he was out cycling. He could be having **the** most pants-soilingly horrendous day of his life and all it would take to cheer him up would be a quick whizz round the block on his bike. It never failed to lift Norm's flagging spirits if only temporarily.

But Norm's spirits weren't in need of lifting at all today as he skidded to a halt in Mikey's drive, where Mikey was busy fiddling about with his own bike.

"Hi, Norm," said Mikey looking up.

"WHAT?" yelled Norm.

Mikey mimed taking headphones out of his ears.

"WHAT?" yelled Norm again, before eventually twigging and taking them out.

"I just said hi," said Mikey.

"Oh, right," said Norm. "Hi."

"What's happening?"

Norm shrugged. "Nothing much."

"Same," said Mikey."

Conversation apparently exhausted, Mikey looked at Norm. "So?"

"So, what?" said Norm.

"You said you were going to tell me why you're in such a good mood?"

"Oh, right," said Norm. "You'll never guess."

"You're right, Norm. I won't. So why don't you just tell me?"

"'Kay," said Norm. "Chelsea's moving."

Mikey looked puzzled. "You mean moving *house*?"

"What?" said Norm. "No, I just mean she's moving."

"Uh?"

"Of *course* I mean she's moving house, you doughnut!"

"Whoa," said Mikey.

"Tell me about it," said Norm.

"When?"

"Dunno."

"Whoa."

"I know."

"Where's she moving **to**?" said Mikey.

Norm shrugged. "Dunno. She could move to Antarctica for all I flipping care."

Mikey didn't say anything and looked like he was letting the news slowly sink in. The news still hadn't **totally** sunk in with **Norm** yet. But it was **beginning** to. And the future was looking bright. Dazzlingly bright. **So** bright, Norm was going to have to take extra care to look where he was going.

"Hello, Norman," said a friendly sounding voice.

Norm spun round to see Mikey's mum standing at the front door.

"Hi, Mikey's mum."

Mikey's mum smiled, as she always did when Norm called her that. And Norm had been calling her that for a very long time now. Since he'd first learned to speak all those years ago. When he and Mikey used to play with each other at parent and toddler group.

"How are things?"

"Things are good, thanks," said Norm.

"Excellent," said Mikey's mum. "How about you, Mikey?"

Mikey sighed. "**Not** so good, Mum."

"Aw, that's a shame," said Mikey's mum. "Why not?"

"Can't fix my bike."

Actually, thought Norm, that really **wasn't** good. Because unless Mikey **did** fix his bike, it looked like it might well have been a wasted journey.

"I've got an idea," said Mikey's mum.

Mikey pulled a face. "Really? But **you** don't know anything about bikes, Mum!"

"Very true," said Mikey's mum. "But I **do** know something about hot chocolate."

"Yessss!" said Norm punching the air. Perhaps it hadn't been **quite** such a wasted journey after all.

Mikey's mum smiled again. "I thought you might like that, Norman."

Might like it? thought Norm. He flipping well **loved** it! Were there supposed to be **seven** wonders of the world? Well there were flipping **eight** if you included Mikey's mum's hot chocolate! It was quite simply **the** most mouth-wateringly delicious thing he'd ever tasted in his life – and that **included**

home-delivered, twelve-inch, deep-crust margherita from Wikipizza with garlic bread **and** potato wedges with spicy dip. **That's** how good Mikey's mum's hot chocolate was. It was beyond awesome. It was...it was... it was... Actually, thought Norm, he couldn't think what it was. But whatever it was, it was flipping brilliant.

"I'll call you when it's ready," said Mikey's mum disappearing inside the house again.

"Thanks, Mum," said Mikey.

"Yeah, thanks, Mikey's mum." Norm grinned.

Mikey sighed as he turned his attention back to his bike.

"So," said Norm. "Brakes, huh?"

Mikey nodded forlornly.

"What's up with them?"

"If I knew **that** I might be able to **fix** them!" snapped Mikey.

There was a deathly silence. By Mikey's standards this had been quite an outburst. In fact, by **Mikey's** standards this had been the equivalent of a volcano suddenly erupting after lying dormant for a couple of hundred thousand years or so. Mikey was usually so calm and laid-back. It was normally **Norm** who blew up out of the blue for no reason whatsoever. Not that Mikey had actually blown up. It had been more like a bit of unexpected turbulence than an actual explosion. But that wasn't the point. The point was that it had been so completely out of character. And they **both** knew it.

"Pardon me for flipping **breathing**," said Norm eventually.

"Sorry, Norm," said Mikey sheepishly.

Norm regarded his best friend for a second. He could tell that Mikey was genuinely apologetic. But what on **earth** had got into him? It was like he'd been momentarily possessed by someone entirely different. Someone who Norm didn't recognise at all. Someone who Norm didn't particularly **want** to recognise, either. Luckily, though, whoever it was seemed to have cleared off again. Mikey was back in the room. Not that they were actually **in** a room. They were actually still on the drive outside Mikey's house. But that wasn't the point, either. The point was...

"Dunno what came over me," said Mikey before Norm could think what the point was.

"'S'all right," said Norm.

"No, Norm," said Mikey emphatically. "It's **not** all right. It's not all right at all."

Norm shrugged. "Whatever."

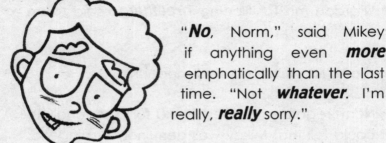

"**No**, Norm," said Mikey if anything even **more** emphatically than the last time. "Not **whatever**. I'm really, **really** sorry."

Norm wasn't sure what to say. So he said nothing.

"I think it must be my hormones or something."

Gordon flipping **Bennet**, thought Norm. Why did Mikey always have to bring up his **hormones?** Just because **he'd** actually **turned** thirteen didn't mean he had to suddenly start talking like a flipping **biology** teacher. Because **Norm** hadn't turned thirteen yet. And frankly, if this was a sign of things to come, he was in no particular **hurry** to turn thirteen, either. It could flipping well wait!

"Norm?"

"Yeah?"

"I said I think it must be my hormones, or something."

"Shut **up**, Mikey! I heard you the *first* time!"

"Pardon?"

"Well, it's disgusting, all that stuff!" said Norm.

Mikey looked puzzled. "No, it's not."

"Er, yeah it *is*," said Norm.

"I think you'll find it's just basic human nature, Norm."

"I think you'll find it's completely flipping **gross**, Mikey!"

"We'll just have to agree to differ," said Mikey.

"What?" said Norm.

"Just accept that one of us thinks one thing – and one of us thinks another."

"Fair enough," said Norm. "But I'm right."

Mikey laughed. "Sorry about the brakes."

"What?" said Norm. "Oh, right."

"I wanted to go biking as well, you know, Norm."

Norm shrugged. "It's not **your** fault."

"Yeah, I know," said Mikey. "I just **wish** I could do something about it!"

Norm grinned. "Do I look like a flipping fairy godmother, or something?"

"What?" said Mikey.

"I can't grant **wishes**, Mikey!"

"Yeah, I know but..."

"You could always just google it."

Mikey looked at Norm.

"What?"

"Just google how to fix your brakes."

"Brilliant, Norm," said Mikey incredulously. "That's a *great* idea!"

Norm pulled a face. Anybody would think he'd just discovered a brand new flipping number or something. It was common sense. You needed to know something? You just flipping googled it! It wasn't even a *remotely* big deal. Norm had been known to google what *time* it was, before

Google

what time is it?

now. It was hardly flipping rocket science. In fact, if Norm ever wanted to actually find out what rocket science was, he'd probably just google it. Not that **that** was ever likely to happen. Norm had about as much interest in rocket science as he had in the origins of lawn mowers, or the history of flipping doors. In other words, none whatso-flipping-ever.

"To the googlemobile!" said Mikey like a superhero, abandoning his bike on the drive and heading into the house.

Gordon flipping Bennet, thought Norm traipsing slowly after him.

CHAPTER 6

"Are you up there, boys?" called Mikey's mum from the bottom of the stairs.

Norm and Mikey were indeed **up there**. To be precise, they were in Mikey's bedroom where they were both huddled round Mikey's iPad. Which was naturally just that little bit better than Norm's **own** iPad. Not that that was Mikey's fault, of course, any more than it was Mikey's fault that he was just that little bit better than Norm at...well, pretty much everything. **Including** biking. **And** he had a slightly better bike than Norm.

Which Norm found particularly annoying and particularly unfair, what with **him** being the one who was completely and utterly bonkers about biking – not Mikey. Yes, Mikey **liked** biking. Just not with the same intensity and passion as Norm. But then, very few people liked biking with the same intensity and passion as Norm.

"Boys?" called Mikey's mum again when neither of them answered.

"Yeah, sorry, we're up here, Mum!" called Mikey.

"Yeah, sorry, Mikey's mum!" called Norm.

Mikey's mum appeared in the doorway a few moments later, a mug in each hand. Not just **any** old mugs either. Massive mugs. Massive mugs topped with towering spirals of squirty cream.

Towering spirals of squirty cream scattered with hundreds of chocolate sprinkles – and with a whacking great chocolate flake sticking out.

"Mmmmm," said Mikey.

"Come to Daddy!" murmured Norm, his stomach immediately beginning to rumble like a distant clap of thunder.

"Sounds like you're ready for this, Norman!" Mikey's mum laughed, plonking the two mugs down on the table.

Ready for it? thought Norm. Oh, he was ready for it all right. He was ready for a mug of Mikey's mum's awesome hot chocolate 24-flipping-7!

"Thanks, Mum," said Mikey.

"Yeah, thanks, Mikey's mum," said Norm dreamily.

"You're very welcome." Mikey's mum laughed. "**_Both_** of you."

Norm picked up one of the mugs and inhaled deeply for a moment, savouring the magnificent chocolatey smell, before taking a gulp. And then another. And then another. And then another. In next to no time he'd polished off the lot. Including the flake.

Mikey's mum smiled.
"What kept you?"

"What?" said
Norm. "I mean,
pardon?"

"I'm just teasing,"
said Mikey's mum. "I've
never **_seen_** anyone drink
a mug of hot chocolate
that fast before!"

"Oh, right," said Norm.

"Do your parents not feed you?"

Norm briefly thought about saying no, on the off chance that Mikey's mum might report his mum and dad for neglect and end up adopting him. He wasn't sure how Mikey would feel about suddenly having a brother after all this time being an only child. It was bound to be a bit weird at first. Then again, thought Norm, *he* wasn't sure how he'd feel about suddenly having *three* brothers instead of just two. Yes Mikey and he were best friends. Always had been. Probably always *would* be. But how would they get on actually *living* together under the same roof? Even a whacking great *big* roof, like Mikey's! Not that it was actually *Mikey's* roof,

of course. Technically it was his mum and dad's roof. But that wasn't the point. The point was that it was a flipping sight bigger than the roof on top of the stupid little house where **Norm** lived. But even so, there was no actual guarantee that he and Mikey would get on with each other. What if they got on each other's **nerves?** What if one of them wanted to watch one thing on TV but the other wanted to watch something else? What if they ended up arguing about who was supposed to be doing the washing up and who was supposed to be sorting out the flipping recycling? It was a load of ifs and buts, thought Norm. But one thing was for sure. If it meant drinking Mikey's mum's hot chocolate every day of the week, he was definitely willing to give it a shot!

"I'm just teasing again, Norman," said Mikey's mum.

"What?" said Norm distractedly.

"How are they, by the way?"

"Who?"

"Your mum and dad?"

"Pfffffff," said Norm. "How long have you got?"

"What do you mean?"

Norm thought for a moment. It was a good question actually. What *did* he mean? Did he mean that his parents drove him round the flipping bend, with their constant commands and continuous nagging? Did he mean that he never got a moment's flipping peace because he was always being told to do *something* or other? Did he mean that his stupid little brothers *never* got told to do stuff? That *he* was always being blamed for stuff that *they* did? That his mum and dad never seemed to listen to a flipping word he said? That *he* never got anything he wanted, but Brian and Dave got *everything* they wanted? That, basically – *everything* was just *so* flipping unfair?

"Norman?"

"Yeah?" said Norm, suddenly snapping out of it.

"Are they *well?*"

"Who?"

Mikey's mum laughed. "Your mum and dad!"

"Oh, right," said Norm. "Yeah. S'pose so."

"You *suppose* so?"

Norm nodded.

"Hmmm."

Norm looked at Mikey's mum. What was she thinking? What exactly was that *hmmm* supposed to mean?

"You know something, Norman?"

"Yeah?" said Norm. "I mean, no. I mean, what?"

"Mikey and I don't *always* see eye to eye. Do we, Mikey?"

76

"What?" said Mikey. "Er, no. Not always, no."

"Really?" said Norm doubtfully.

"Really!" said Mikey's mum. "You look surprised."

Norm wasn't **surprised**. He was abso-flipping-lutely flabbergasted. Because as far as **he** knew, Mikey and his mum **never** argued. About **anything**. Or at least, if they **did**, he'd never actually **seen** them arguing. He just couldn't imagine it – let alone imagine what they could possibly find to argue **about**. Mikey was an only child. **He** didn't get blamed for stuff he hadn't done. Plus he lived in a whacking great big house. Well, a fairly **average** sized house actually. But bigger than **Norm's** glorified rabbit hutch, anyway. Then again, what wasn't? **And** both of Mikey's parents had jobs. So money **clearly** wasn't a problem. He'd never seen supermarket own brand **anything** in **Mikey's** house. Not like his **own** house. **Everything** was flipping own brand in his **own** house, thought Norm bitterly. He wouldn't be surprised if the actual *house* was flipping **own** brand.

"**Everybody** argues from time to time," said Mikey's mum as if she'd been reading Norm's mind.

Yeah, thought Norm. From time to flipping **time**. Not **all** the flipping time, like he and **his** parents did! They argued about everything it was **possible** to argue about. What time it was. What day it was. Heck, even what **year** it was. **Nothing** was off-limits when it came to disagreeing with **his** mum and dad.

Norm's phone rang. He glanced at Mikey's mum.

"Go ahead," she said. "Don't mind me."

"Hello?" said Norm answering. "Oh, hi, Dad."

Norm listened for a moment before pulling a face.

"What? But..."

Norm sighed a sigh which, even by *his* standards, sounded particularly world weary.

"'Kay, Dad. Bye."

"What is it?" said Mikey as Norm ended the call and pocketed his phone again.

"Gotta go," said Norm getting up.

"Why?"

"He didn't say," said Norm dejectedly. "All I know is I've got to go home."

"But..."

"What?"

"I wanted to..."

"What?" said Norm.

It was Mikey's turn to sigh. It looked like whatever it

was that he wanted to do was just going to have to wait.

"Nothing."

"'Kay. See you later, then, Mikey," said Norm heading off.

"See you later, Norm," said Mikey.

"Bye, Mikey's mum. Thanks for the hot chocolate."

"You're very welcome, Norman," said Mikey's mum. "Pity you only drank half of it."

Norm stopped and turned around.

"Pardon?"

"The other half's all over your face!"

Norm glanced in the mirror hanging on the back of the door. Mikey's mum was exaggerating. But not by much. The other half of the hot chocolate wasn't exactly *all* over his face – but there was a thick brown line around his mouth, like badly applied lipstick. Not that Norm had ever actually **applied** lipstick before. Badly or otherwise. And even if he **had**, it certainly wouldn't have been **brown** lipstick. But he got the point. All he needed was a red nose and a pair of massive shoes and he'd look like a flipping clown.

"Don't go kissing any girls now!" Mikey's mum laughed as Norm disappeared down the stairs.

Right, thought Norm. Like **that** was going to happen. Now, or flipping **ever!**

CHAPTER 7

By the time Norm had cycled home again he'd licked every last bit of hot chocolate off his face. Despite that, though, he **still** had a bad taste in his mouth as he got off his bike and leaned it against the wall. Why on **earth** had he had to come back from Mikey's so flipping **soon?** It was Saturday afternoon, for goodness sake! And Saturday afternoons were meant for one thing and one thing alone. Biking. And chilling. OK, so technically that was actually two things, thought Norm. But that wasn't the point. The point was that he should have been out and about enjoying himself. But oh no. His dad wouldn't let him do **that**, would he? That would

never flipping do. Never mind the fact that Norm might actually have been having flipping ***fun***. Had his *dad* never had fun when **he** was young? If his dad had ever actually ***been*** young. It was hard to imagine.

"In here!" called Norm's dad as Norm opened the front door and stepped into the hallway.

"Where?" said Norm closing the door behind him.

"Front room!"

Gordon flipping Bennet, thought Norm. The front room? That didn't sound good, for a flipping start. It was the equivalent of being summoned to the head teacher's office for a rocketing. Not that Norm had ever actually ***been*** summoned to the head teacher's office for a rocketing. Or at least, not yet he hadn't, anyway. But there was still plenty of time for that to happen.

"Now!" bellowed Norm's dad.

Norm sighed as he prepared to face the music. At least he **assumed** he was about to face the music anyway. But precisely what **kind** of music? If the tone of Norm's dad's voice was anything to go by, it sounded like it was going to be pretty heavy.

"What have you got to say about **that?**" said Norm's dad the split second Norm poked his head tentatively round the door.

Norm pulled a face.

"About **what?**"

"What do you mean, about **what?**" said Norm's dad, his voice getting higher and the vein on the side of his head already beginning to throb. Both of which were tell-tale signs that Norm's dad was getting stressed. Not that Norm ever noticed. But then Norm wouldn't have noticed if a penguin had walked into the room and asked who'd ordered a taxi.

"About *that!*" said Norm's dad with a tilt of his head towards the coffee table in front of him.

"The table?" said Norm.

"No!" said Norm's dad. "About what's *on* the table!"

Norm looked, but the only thing he could see actually *on* the table was a small, square-shaped glass bottle.

"Well?" said Norm's dad.

Norm was genuinely unsure what he was expected to say. What *could* he say? It was just a flipping bottle. A flipping bottle he'd never even *seen* before. Or at least, Norm didn't *think* he'd seen it before, anyway.

"*Well?*" said Norm's dad again, the vein on the side of his head starting to throb faster and faster. Not that Norm noticed.

"Erm. It's very nice?"

Norm's dad looked at Norm for a moment. "Yes it **is** very nice, Norman."

Was that all it was, then? thought Norm. Had he passed the test? And if so, could he go now?

"Any idea how long I've had it?"

Had **what?** thought Norm. A terrible fashion sense? An appalling taste in music? Breath like a constipated camel's?

"The **aftershave**, Norman!" said Norm's dad as if he knew exactly what Norm had been thinking.

So **that's** what it was, thought Norm. Aftershave. How on earth was he supposed to know **that?** He had no need for flipping **aftershave!** He was nearly **thirteen**. Not nearly **thirty!** There was more fuzz on a baby's bum than there was on his flipping **chin!**

"I'll tell you, shall I?" said Norm's dad without waiting for an answer. "Seventeen years."

Phwoar, thought Norm. Seventeen year old aftershave? In that case it must be **well** past its smell-by date!

"Seventeen years, four months and three days to be precise."

Uh? thought Norm. How come he knew **exactly** how long he'd had the aftershave? He'd always known his dad was **weird**. But he had no idea he was **that** weird.

"Beast," said Norm's dad.

"Sorry, what?" said Norm getting more confused by the second.

"That's the name of the aftershave. Or, to give it it's full title, Beast **Pour Homme**."

"Poor what?"

"It's French," said Norm's dad. "It just means 'for men'."

"Right," said Norm who had no idea there was even such a **thing** as aftershave for women.

"It means a lot to me."

"What does?"

"The **aftershave**, Norman! What do you **think** I mean?"

Norm shrugged. He genuinely had no flipping **idea** what his dad meant. He certainly had no flipping idea where this was all heading. If indeed it was heading anywhere. For all Norm knew, his dad might just be having one of his random rants. On the other hand, he **could** be having some kind of midlife meltdown. Either way he was very angry. And it appeared to have

something to do with the aftershave. Although quite how **Norm** was involved in any of this was anybody's guess. Because Norm didn't have a flipping **clue**.

"It's got…"

"What?" said Norm when it became clear that his dad wasn't going to finish the sentence without some kind of prompting.

"Sentimental value."

"Right," said Norm.

Norm's dad glared at Norm for a few moments.

"Which is why I'm so…"

Annoying? thought Norm.

"Upset," said Norm's dad.

Norm replayed the conversation, in his head. Was he missing something here? Had he actually dropped off for a second? Had someone

accidentally pressed **fast forward?** Because he **still** hadn't got the faintest idea what any of this had to do with **him**.

"Why did you throw it away, Norman?"

"Sorry, what?" said Norm.

"Why did you throw it away?"

"I **didn't**," said Norm.

"Yes, you **did**," said Norm's dad. "You threw it out for recycling."

"I did?" said Norm.

"Yes, Norman," said Norm's dad. "You **did**."

"Right."

Norm's dad looked at Norm. "Right?"

Norm nodded.

"**Right?**"

Norm nodded again.

"Is that all you've got to say?" said Norm's dad. "Right?"

thought Norm. If he nodded one more time his head was going to come off.

"Why, Norman?"

"Why what?"

"Why did you **do** it?" said Norm's dad, his voice getting even higher.

"I didn't **mean** to, Dad."

"I should hope **not!**"

"I didn't even know I *had*."

Norm's dad huffed. "Well, I must say I find *that* hard to believe!"

"Must you?" muttered Norm under his breath.

"What was that, Norman?"

"Nothing," said Norm, beginning to realise that *this* was the reason he'd had to cut short his whole flipping afternoon! The afternoon he *should* have spent biking with Mikey. Well, once Mikey had sorted his brakes out, anyway. But that wasn't the point. The point was...

"The point *is*," said Norm's dad, "you need to start paying more *attention*, Norman!"

Norm sighed. As far as he was concerned, this wasn't merely grossly *unfair*, it was also grossly *stupid*. Even if he *had* seen the aftershave when he was doing the recycling there would have been no reason to *not* chuck it out with the rest of the stuff. How was *he* supposed to know that it meant a lot to his dad? How was *he* supposed to know

that it had flipping **sentimental** value or whatever?
How was **he** supposed to know that his dad was
going to go utterly ape-bonkers-ballistic and
completely **overreact** like this? It
was just some stupid little
bottle. It wasn't like he'd
accidentally chucked
out something really
valuable!

"Norman?"

"Sorry, what?" said
Norm distractedly.

"That's exactly what I
mean!"

Norm pulled a face.

"You need to start paying more **attention!**"

"But..."

"But **nothing**, Norman!" said Norm's dad. "You
should pay more attention. End of!"

Norm sighed **again**. He wished it was the end of the flipping **conversation**.

"And stop sighing like that!"

"Like what?"

"**That!**" squeaked Norm's dad like a mouse with tonsillitis.

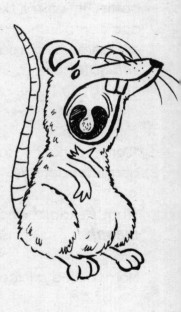

Norm couldn't help sniggering.

"What's so funny?"

"Nothing," said Norm.

Norm's dad fixed Norm with a glare. "You're banned, by the way."

"Banned?" said Norm.

Norm's dad nodded.

"Banned from **what?**"

Norm's dad stroked his chin thoughtfully. "I haven't decided yet."

"What?" said Norm.

"I'll let you know once I've decided."

"Can you give me a clue?"

"No, I **can't** give you a clue, Norman! What do you think this **is?** Some kind of TV quiz show or something?"

Norm thought for a moment. If this **was** some kind of TV show it would be a pretty flipping **rubbish** one.

"But..."

"But **nothing!**" said Norm's dad. "I'll let you **know** once I've **decided**."

Norm did his best to try and get his head round what had just happened but it wasn't easy. As far as he could make out, he'd just been banned from something or other for **doing** something he didn't even know he'd **done** until just now. Not only **that** but he'd had to come home **early** to be told that he'd been banned from something or other for doing something he didn't even know he'd done until just now. And why **couldn't** his dad tell him what he was banned from? thought Norm. If **that** wasn't a breach of human rights he'd like to know what flipping **was!**

"Can I ask a question, Dad?"

"Depends," said Norm's dad.

"On what?" said Norm.

"On what it is."

Gordon flipping Bennet, thought Norm. How could his dad know what the question was unless he flipping well **asked** it? This was getting ridiculous. In fact, never mind **getting** ridiculous. It had already **got** ridiculous and was becoming something else entirely. Something that was **way** beyond anything *Norm* could comprehend.

"Well?" said Norm's dad.

"What?" said Norm.

"What's your question?"

"Oh right, yeah, " said Norm. "How do you know?"

"How do I know what?"

"How do you know I...chucked out your aftershave?" said Norm deliberately omitting the word **accidentally** from the sentence. There was no point. He was going to get the flipping blame anyway. In fact, he already **had**. Same as flipping always.

"That's for me to know and you to find out."

And exactly what was **that** supposed to mean? wondered Norm who was beginning to suspect that his dad was talking in riddles just to annoy him. Honestly, it was like trying to have a conversation with a flipping **wizard** or something.

"Off you go," said Norm's dad with a dismissive wave of his hand.

"What?" said Norm.

"You can go now."

Norm looked puzzled. "You mean back to Mikey's?"

"No, I do **not** mean back to Mikey's!" said Norm's dad. "I mean up to your **room!**"

"But..." began Norm.

"In fact, that's it," said Norm's dad. "I've decided."

"What?" said Norm.

"**That's** what you're banned from. Going to Mikey's."

"But..."

"What have I told you about **buts**, Norman?"

There was a sudden burst of laughter. Norm turned round to see his little brother standing in the doorway.

"That's funny!" said Dave.

"What is?" said Norm irritably.

"What's dad told you about butts?"

"What?" said Norm. "No, not **those** kind of buts, Dave, you doughnut!"

"Oh, right," said Dave heading for the stairs. "Still funny, though."

Norm sighed.

"**Stop** sighing!" said Norm's dad.

"Gordon flipping Bennet," muttered Norm.

"And stop saying that, as well!"

Gordon flipping Bennet, thought Norm. Stop doing this. Stop doing that. Stop doing the other. At this rate he'd be lucky if he was allowed to flipping **breathe!**

"Off you go now," said Norm's dad. "Chop, chop!"

"Gladly," muttered Norm getting up.

"What was that, Norman?"

"Nothing," said Norm.

CHAPTER 8

Norm stomped up the stairs in a filthy mood. He still couldn't quite believe that the **only** flipping reason his Saturday afternoon had been so **rudely** interrupted and completely flipping **ruined** was because he'd thrown out some stupid aftershave. Not even on purpose. **Accidentally** thrown out some stupid aftershave! What was the big deal about **that?** He wouldn't have minded **quite** so much if it had been a **half** decent reason. If the house had been on fire, for instance. **That** would have been a half decent reason.

Actually, thought Norm that would have been **more** than half a decent reason. That would have been more like a three **quarters** decent reason. But even then he'd have still been a **bit** miffed at missing out on any potential biking action. At least he'd have **begun** to understand why he'd suddenly had to come home, though. And on the plus side, if the house really **had** been on fire there'd have been a reasonable chance of having to move to another one. Hopefully to somewhere a bit bigger and better this time. Not that **that** would be very difficult. Pretty much **anywhere** would be bigger and better than **this** stupid little house.

What made things even **worse**, as far as Norm was concerned, was that his dad had somehow got his precious aftershave **back**. It wasn't like it had been chucked out and lost **forever**. It wasn't going to be discovered and dug up on some boring TV programme two hundred years from now. Not that

THE HISTORY OF

Tomato Soup

SOUP

Norm would ever watch a flipping programme like **that**. Firstly, he'd sooner watch a programme about the history of flipping soup. Secondly, there probably wouldn't *be* TV two hundred years from now. And thirdly, even if there **was**, Norm would be nearly 213 by then.

What was so special about the aftershave, anyway? **That's** what Norm didn't get. Well, **one** of the things he didn't get. But honestly, if it meant **that** much to his dad he could always go out and get some more, couldn't he? What was the flipping problem? Because as far as Norm could see, there **wasn't** one.

Norm stopped at the top of the stairs and sniffed. He'd caught a whiff of something. But what? He couldn't quite put his finger on it. Not only that but he was pretty sure he didn't **want** to put his finger on it either. Or put anything **else** on it, for that matter. Because whatever it was, it stank like a ping pong player's armpit. Not that Norm had ever got close enough to actually **smell** a ping pong player's armpit, of course.

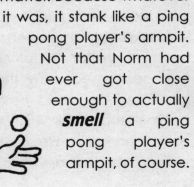

And with luck he never would.

Pausing outside the bathroom door, Norm sniffed again. But surprisingly, **that** wasn't where the smell was coming from. This wasn't some kind of toiletty whiff. And frankly, if it **had** been, then whoever was responsible for it had got something **seriously** wrong with them and was possibly in need of **urgent** medical attention.

Either that or a gerbil had somehow found its way into their pants drawer and then died.

It wasn't as if Norm was particularly **desperate** to discover what the stink was – or where it was coming from. But he was **vaguely** curious. And it wasn't as if he had anything **better** to do. Actually, as far as Norm was concerned, now that he could no longer go biking he didn't have **anything** to do, full flipping stop. But it wasn't like he had some kind of fascination or lifelong **passion** for pongs. He wasn't weird or anything. He didn't see himself lying on a psychiatrist's couch when he was older, hoping to get to the **bottom** of the problem. No pun intended.

There was a sudden woofing sound from Brian and Dave's room.

Stupid flipping dog, thought Norm. And, for that matter, stupid flipping **brothers** too. Why couldn't his dad have dropped them off at the pool and just flipping **left** them there? That way he could have at least **imagined** he was an only child again. For a little while, at least. Until the swimming pool phoned. Or the police came round or whatever. Was that **really** too much to ask? Apparently it **was**.

There was more woofing. Before he knew what he was doing – or even **why** he was doing it – Norm had opened the door and walked in. It took about a thousandth of a second to wish that he hadn't. Not only had the stench suddenly got a whole lot worse, but there, sitting on a chair like some kind of canine movie star, was John. Standing in front of him and holding up a mirror was Dave. Standing behind him was Brian.

"What are you **doing?**" said Norm.

"Holding up a mirror," said Dave as if this was the stupidest question ever.

"I can see **that**," said Norm. "But **why?**"

"So John can see his reflection!" said Dave as if this was the **second** most stupid question ever.

"Gordon flipping Bennet," said Norm. "I know what flipping **mirrors** are for, Dave, you little freak. I'm not **stupid**."

"We're just giving him a makeover," explained Brian.

"A **what?**" said Norm.

"A makeover," said Brian.

Norm suddenly realised that Brian was holding something too.

"Are those..."

"Mum's hair straighteners?" said Brian. "Yes, they are actually."

"But..."

"What?"

"It's **supposed** to be curly!" said Norm. "It's a flipping... cockadoodledoo, or whatever!"

"You mean a cock-a-poo?" said Dave.

"Yeah, that," said Norm.

"So?" said Brian. "We're just giving him a new look, that's all."

"Gordon flipping Bennet," muttered Norm.

"What's wrong with *that?*" said Brian.

"What's *wrong* with that?" said Norm beginning to get seriously wound up. "It's a flipping *dog!*"

"Yeah? So?" said Brian.

"So you can't give a dog a new *look*, Brian!"

"Oh, really?" said Brian.

"Yeah, really," said Norm.

"What are you going to make it look *like?* A flipping *zebra?*"

Brian pulled a face. "Don't be **silly**, Norman."

"It's not **me** being silly!"
said Norm.

"Yes, it is," said Brian.

Norm sighed. There was
no point trying to argue,
though. Well there **was**. He
just couldn't be bothered,
that was all.

"And it's **he**, by the way."

"What?" said Norm.

"John's a **he**, not an **it**," said Brian.

John responded by turning round and licking Brian
full in the face.

"Yes, you **are**, aren't you, boy?" cooed Brian in a
squeaky baby voice.

"That is dis-flipping-**gusting**," said Norm.

Brian shrugged. "I don't mind."

"What?" said Norm. "No, I mean it's disgusting for the dog, not **you!**"

"What?" said Brian.

"Well, I wouldn't want to lick you," said Norm. "You never know **what** you might catch."

Dave laughed, but Brian ignored Norm's insult and started straightening John's curls instead. Or at least he **tried** to straighten them.

Norm watched his brothers and shook his head in exasperation. Why on **earth** would anyone in their right mind want to give a flipping **dog** a flipping makeover? Then again, thought Norm, why on earth would anyone in their right mind want a flipping **dog** in the first flipping place? Because as far as he could see, all dogs ever did was eat, sleep, poop and sniff other dogs' bums. But despite that, Brian and Dave had wanted one. And as flipping usual, if Brian and Dave wanted something, Brian and Dave usually flipping got it. Which was the complete and utter opposite of Norm, who never, ever got anything **he** flipping wanted. It was so unfair.

Norm exhaled slowly and noisily before inhaling again. And then it suddenly hit him, like an out of control toddler in a toy shop. The source of the stink was John! Of course it was! Why hadn't he realised before?

"Phwoar!"

"What's the matter?" said Dave.

Norm was incredulous. "What's the **matter?**"

Dave nodded.

"Can you not **smell** that?"

"Smell what?" said Dave.

"You're joking, right?" said Norm.

Dave shook his head. Evidently he **wasn't** joking.

"I think he means the aftershave, Dave," said Brian casually.

Norm looked at Brian for a moment. "What did you just say?"

"I said I think you mean the aftershave."

Norm was slowly but surely beginning to put two and two together. But it was taking some time. The fumes were clearly beginning to affect him. Much more of this and he was going to start hallucinating pink rabbits and tap-dancing badgers.

"*Aftershave?*"

Brian nodded.

"You put **aftershave** on a **dog?**" said Norm. "Seriously?"

"Why not?" said Brian as if this was the most natural thing in the world and not, as Norm clearly seemed to think, completely unnatural.

"What aftershave?" said Norm.

"Dad's aftershave," said Brian.

"Obviously," said Norm.

"What?" said Brian.

"Well, I mean obviously it's **Dad's** aftershave, Brian, you idiot! No one else round here shaves, do they?"

"I'm not an idiot," said Brian indignantly.

"Which aftershave?" said Norm. "And yeah, you

are, by the way."

"Just ordinary aftershave," said Dave quickly, before Brian could say anything else. "Nothing special."

Norm narrowed his eyes and gave his youngest brother a look. Why had he felt the need to say **that?**

"Nothing **special**, Dave?"

"Yeah," said Dave. "I mean, no. I mean..."

"It's not...Beans **Pour Homme**, by any chance, is it?" said Norm struggling to remember the name his dad had said only a few minutes previously.

"**Beans Pour Homme?**" said Dave. "Don't you mean **Beast Pour Homme?**"

Dave was right, thought Norm. He **had** meant **Beast Pour Homme. Beans Pour Homme** would have been even **smellier!**

"So you've heard of it, then?"

Dave shrugged. "I'm not sure. I might have done."

"You **might** have done?" said Norm.

"He's just..." began Brian.

"I'm not talking to you, Brian. I'm talking to Dave."

"I just think..."

"Shut up, Brian!" said Norm. "I don't flipping *care* what you think!"

"Right, I'm telling," said Brian.

"Don't care," said Norm.

Brian looked confused.

"What?"

"I'm already banned from going to Mikey's," said Norm.

"Oh," said Brian. "That's a pity."

"You're flipping *right* it's a flipping pity!" said Norm. "We were supposed to be going biking!"

"What?" said Brian. "No, I meant that's a pity because I was looking forward to *telling*."

Norm sighed. There was only so much of this he could take. And he'd very nearly exceeded his limit. Not just for the day. For the rest of his life.

"And anyway," said Brian.

"What?" snapped Norm irritably.

"What's this got to do with *us?*"

It was a good question, actually, thought Norm. What *had* it got to do with his brothers? He was no detective, but if this didn't have *something* to do with them he'd personally give John a full body massage *and* trim his flipping fingernails. Or pawnails, or whatever they were flipping called.

"I've just remembered something," said Dave putting down the mirror and heading for the door.

"What?" said Norm.

"Erm, I've forgotten," said Dave sheepishly.

"Uh?" said Norm. "You've **_forgotten_** what you just **_remembered?_**'

But it was too late. Dave had already disappeared. And as far as Norm was concerned, he'd disappeared in a bit too much of a hurry.

CHAPTER 9

By the time Norm caught up with his little brother, Dave was already kicking a football round the back garden. Which was a laugh for a start, as far as Norm was concerned. Back *garden?* He'd seen bigger flipping tea towels. There wasn't room to swing a *hamster*, let alone a flipping *cat.* Not that they actually *had* a hamster, of course. Or a cat, for that matter. But that wasn't the point. The point was it was a ridiculously tiny garden. But at least it was bigger than the so-called *front* garden, which made the *back* garden seem like a flipping safari park by comparison.

"Remembered yet?" said Norm.

"Who? Me?" said Dave looking up.

"Who do you **think** I was talking to?" said Norm. "The flipping garden gnome?"

Dave glanced at the gnome in question, sitting behind some kind of scrawny looking bush and fishing in a non-existent pond.

"Graham?"

Norm pulled a face. "What?"

"Graham," repeated Dave. "That's what I call the gnome."

"You've got a **name** for the gnome?" said Norm.

Dave shrugged. "Why not?"

Gordon flipping Bennet, thought Norm. Just when you thought that **nothing** could be weirder than giving a dog a flipping makeover.

"Why Graham?"

Dave shrugged again. "Starts with a 'g'."

"Yeah, so?" said Norm.

"So does **gnome**."

"Uh? What? No it **doesn't**, Dave, you doughnut. **Gnome** starts with an 'n'. Obviously."

"Nah, it doesn't," said Dave. "Starts with a 'g'. Trust me."

"A 'g'?"

"It's silent."

"What?" said Norm getting more and more confused. "Course it's flipping silent! It's a **gnome**, Dave! A **plastic** gnome!"

"But..."

"I hate to break this to you, Dave – but it's not actually a **real** gnome."

"I meant the 'g' is silent."

"What?" said Norm.

"The 'g' is silent," said Dave. "In **gnome**."

"Oh, right," said Norm finally twigging what Dave meant. "I knew that."

They looked at each other for a moment. Norm knew that Dave didn't believe him. Not only that but Dave knew that Norm knew that he didn't believe him. Not only **that** but Norm knew that Dave knew that Norm knew that he didn't believe him. But right now Norm didn't care. He'd followed his little brother into this sorry excuse for a garden for one particular reason. And it certainly wasn't to have a flipping English lesson. **Or** play flipping football.

"So?"

"So, what?" said Dave.

"Have you remembered what you'd forgotten, yet?"

"Erm…"

"See, I've got a theory," said Norm without waiting for Dave to answer.

"Oh yeah?" said Dave casually.

"Yeah," said Norm. "Would you like to hear it?"

"Erm…"

"I'm going to tell you, anyway."

"'Kay."

"I don't actually think you suddenly remembered anything at all just now, Dave," said

Norm. "I think you were just looking for an excuse to leave the room."

"No I wasn't," said Dave.

"Yeah you were," said Norm. "You could see where the conversation was heading."

"I don't know what you're talking about," said Dave looking just about everywhere except directly at Norm.

"I think you **do**, Dave," said Norm. "I think you know **exactly** what I'm talking about."

"I don't," said Dave still managing to avoid any kind of eye contact.

This was going nowhere fast, thought Norm. He needed Dave to **know** that he was deadly serious. That he'd stay out here until Dave spilled the beans. And there were definitely beans to be spilled. Norm knew that his

123

dad hadn't just randomly **found** the aftershave bottle in the recycling bin. Someone had deliberately **planted** it there. And he had a pretty good idea who that **someone** was.

"Fancy a kick about?"

That did the trick. Dave suddenly looked straight at Norm as if Norm had just announced he was doing a sponsored karaoke in aid of homeless llamas. Norm **hated** football and Dave knew it. So if Norm had just suggested a kick about,

Dave knew that he was prepared to go to any lengths – no matter how extreme – to get the information he wanted. The game was up. It was time to come clean.

"OK, OK, it was me!" blurted Dave, finally crumbling under the intense pressure.

Norm was determined

to enjoy this moment and make Dave squirm like a worm on the end of a fishing line.

"Did you hear me?" said Dave. "Brian had nothing to do with it. It was me! I did it!"

Norm stared at his little brother and did his best to smile like an evil baddie in a James Bond movie. But it wasn't easy, what with not having a bald head. Or a gold tooth. Or an evil cat to stroke.

"Did **what** exactly, Dave?"

"I took the aftershave."

"What aftershave?"

"The Beast **Pour Homme**."

"I flipping **knew** it," said Norm.

Dave nodded. "I know you did."

"You know I knew it?" said Norm.

Dave nodded again.

"I know you did," said Norm.

Dave sighed. "I know."

"Where from?"

"Pardon?" said Dave.

"Where did you take the aftershave *from*, Dave?"

Dave hesitated for a moment.

"Dad's drawer."

"Which drawer?" said Norm. "He's got lots of drawers."

"His pants drawer."

"His *pants* drawer?"

"Yeah," said Dave.

126

Norm shuddered. There were some things he just didn't want to **ever** have to think about. And his dad's pants drawer was most definitely one of them.

"So you **knew** that it was special, then?"

Dave pulled a face. "What? Dad's pants drawer?"

"The **aftershave**, you doughnut. If Dad hides something in his pants drawer, he **really** doesn't want anyone finding it!"

"Oh right," said Dave. "Yeah. I knew it must be special."

"Then what?"

Dave shrugged. "We put some on John."

"Yes, obviously," said Norm wanting to cut to the

chase. "But what about **afterwards?**"

"I chucked it in the recycling bin."

"Yes, but **why** did you chuck it in the recycling bin, Dave?"

Dave looked nervously at Norm.

"Well?"

"I knew you'd get the blame."

Well, **that** figured, thought Norm. After all, he'd had a whole **lifetime** of being blamed for stuff he hadn't actually *done*. Well, not a **whole** lifetime. At least, not **yet** he hadn't, anyway. But he'd been blamed for stuff he hadn't done for as long as he could remember. Probably even longer. So you'd think he'd be used to it by now. It was still flipping annoying, though. And *still* flipping unfair.

"I'm sorry, Norman."

"What?" said Norm.

"I said I'm sorry," said Dave. "I shouldn't have done it."

"You're flipping *right* you shouldn't have done it, Dave."

"Yeah well, I was cross, wasn't I?"

"Cross?" said Norm.

"I nearly wet myself."

"Oh and I suppose *that* was my fault, as well, was it?"

"Yeah, it was actually," said Dave.

Uh? thought Norm. Surely not? How could *he* be responsible for his brother losing control of his bodily functions? Or **almost** losing control of his bodily functions, anyway.

"You were taking so long in the toilet!" said Dave. "This morning? Remember?"

"What?" said Norm. "Oh right, yeah."

"I ended up having to pee out here."

"What? In the garden?" said Norm.

"I didn't have a choice!" said Dave.

Norm pulled a face. "What about the kitchen sink?"

"Aw, yuk!" shrieked Dave. "That's **disgusting!**"

"Not if you move the dishes first, it's not," said Norm.

Dave looked horrified.

"I'm **joking**, Dave!" said Norm. "So it was basically revenge, then?"

Dave thought for a moment.

"Yeah, I suppose it was, really."

Norm nodded. He was secretly quite impressed with his little brother. Proud almost. Not that he had any intention of telling him **that** of course. But Dave had clearly thought this through. And now that he'd explained everything, it sounded almost reasonable. Norm was beginning to understand why Dave had done what he'd done.

"Where did you do it?"

"Do what?" said Dave.

"Pee," said Norm.

"Why do you want to know?"

"So I know where not to stand."

"Over there," said Dave. "Near Graham."

"**Near** Graham, or **on** Graham?" said Norm.

"**Near** him!" said Dave emphatically.

"Was the **pee** silent?" chuckled Norm.

"It's not funny!" said Dave. "Someone..."

"What?"

"Saw me."

"Who?" said Norm.

"Chelsea," whispered Dave.

"Why are you whispering, Dave?" said Norm.

"Yes, why **are** you whispering, Dave?" said Chelsea suddenly popping up on the other side of the fence.

"Gordon flipping Bennet," muttered Norm. "What kept you?"

Chelsea smiled sweetly. "Missed you too, **Norman**."

"Have you been listening?"

"To what?"

"Our conversation?"

"Why would I want to listen to **your** conversation?" said Chelsea.

Norm shrugged. "Dunno."

"I think you're confusing me with someone **without** a life, **Norman**."

Dave couldn't help giggling.

"Shut it, you little freak!" hissed Norm.

"**That's** not very nice," said Chelsea.

Norm shrugged. "So?"

"So you should be **nicer**."

"He's **my** flipping brother."

"Doesn't mean you can be **horrible** to him."

Norm sighed. How was it possible to get **so** wound up by one person so flipping quickly?

"Sorry, Dave, by the way," said Chelsea.

"What for?" said Dave.

"You know?" said Chelsea. "When I accidentally caught you having a...."

"Oh right, that," said Dave quickly. "That's OK."

"I didn't mean to embarrass you."

"Wasn't your fault."

"No," said Norm. "Apparently that was **my** fault."

"Really?" said Chelsea. "In that case I think you owe your brother an apology."

"Dream on," muttered Norm.

"How come you haven't moved yet, anyway?" said Dave.

Chelsea laughed. "Steady, Eddie! The sign only went up this morning!"

"Oh, right," said Dave.

"You trying to get rid of me or something?"

Dave was mortified. "No, no, not at all!"

Chelsea waited a couple of seconds before bursting out laughing again. "I'm just pulling your leg, Dave!"

"What?"

"I'm just *joking*."

"Oh right," said Dave, looking and sounding relieved.

"*That* wasn't very nice," said Norm pointedly.

"Oh, I see, so you're *defending* your brother now, are you?" said Chelsea.

"What's it got to do with *you?*" said Norm.

"Oooooooh!" squealed Chelsea sarcastically. "*Someone's* got out the wrong side of bed today, *Norman!*"

Norm sighed. If only he hadn't actually got out of bed at *all*. If only he'd *stayed* in bed, none of this might have flipping *happened!* Then again, if he'd *stayed* in bed he *still* wouldn't have been able to go biking. It was a no-win situation whichever way he flipping looked at it.

"Hello again, Chelsea," said Norm's mum appearing at the back door.

"Hi!" squeaked Chelsea like butter wouldn't melt in her mouth.

"Can I have a quick word, Norm, love?"

"What?" said Norm.

"A quick word, please?"

"'Kay," said Norm showing no sign of moving.

"Inside?"

Norm huffed and puffed as if his mum had just asked him to **_hoover_** the lawn, not just walk **_across_** it. Not that it would have taken very long to hoover the lawn even if she had, what with it only being the size of a flipping postage stamp. But he was secretly quite glad that he

had an excuse to get back inside the house again. Not only was Chelsea driving him round the flipping bend, he'd just remembered that technically he wasn't actually supposed to be *outside* in the first place. He was supposed to be in his *room*. And if his dad saw him out here now he might not be able to go biking tomorrow either. And that really *would* be a flipping disaster!

"Well?" said Norm's mum. "What are you waiting for?"

What was he *waiting* for? thought Norm trudging slowly towards the house. Wasn't it flipping *obvious?* He was waiting for Chelsea to hurry up and flipping move! And the sooner the flipping better!.

CHAPTER 10

"Sit yourself down, love," said Norm's mum when Norm finally managed to drag himself into the kitchen.

Norm did as he was told and sat himself down at the table, opposite his mum. But what was this all about? Surely he wasn't going to be given some other boring job or stupid *chore* to do, was he? Because if so, he might as well have stayed in the so-called flipping *garden* and been slowly *annoyed* to death, by Chelsea. And thinking about it, thought Norm, thinking about it, if he was about to be given some boring job or stupid chore to do, why would his

Here lies Norm IT'S SO UNFAIR.

mum have told him to sit down first? Surely she'd have just told him to do it. It didn't make sense. Then again, in Norm's experience, very little made sense anyway. So no change there then. Unless of course his mum was going to start banging on about flipping homework and stuff? As far as Norm knew, he didn't actually **have** any homework. Not that that had ever stopped his parents banging on about it in the past.

"Don't worry, it's nothing bad," said Norm's mum gently. "At least, I **hope** it isn't, anyway."

Norm looked at his mum for a moment.

"What do you mean?"

"How's Mikey?"

Norm hated it when someone answered a question by asking him another question.

"Is that what you told me to come inside for?" said Norm, completely unaware that **he'd** just answered a question by asking another question. "To ask me how Mikey is?"

"Kind of," said Norm's mum.

Norm pulled a face. "***Kind*** of?"

"Well yes, I suppose it was, really."

"Why?" said Norm.

"Why?" said Norm's mum.

"Yeah," said Norm. "I mean, you could ask me how Mikey is ***anytime***."

"Well..."

"Well, what?" said Norm.

"His mum just called."

"On the phone, you mean?" said Norm, just in case Mikey's mum had, for some reason, decided to *shout* instead.

Norm's mum nodded.

"What for?"

"She was..."

"What?" said Norm beginning to get a bit anxious. Mikey was his best friend, after all. Had something *happened* to him?

"Well, she was wondering if I'd noticed anything... different about Mikey, lately."

Uh? thought Norm. **Different?** What was *that* supposed to mean? Had Mikey grown another head? Had he started speaking Japanese for

no reason whatsoever? Had he suddenly developed an uncontrollable passion for wallpaper?

"Apparently he's not been himself lately."

"Really?" said Norm. "Who **has** he been, then?"

Norm's mum smiled. "I don't think that's quite what she meant."

"Well, what **did** she mean then, Mum?"

Norm's mum thought for a moment.

"I think she thinks he might be a bit...**upset** about something?"

"Upset?" said Norm. "About what?"

"That's what I thought *you* might know, love."

It was **Norm's** turn to think for a moment.

"Well, his brakes aren't working properly."

"Pardon?"

"On his bike."

"Oh, I see," said Norm's mum. "I don't think **that's** what she meant, either."

Come to think of it, thought Norm thinking of it, Mikey **had** suddenly snapped at him earlier on. Of course, he'd tried to blame it on his hormones and all that other gross stuff. But Norm knew deep down that there had to be more to it than **that**. Maybe it was something he'd said or done? Something **Norm** had said or done. Not something **Mikey** had said or done. That would be stupid. But what? What could Norm possibly have said or done that would upset Mikey so much that **Mikey's** mum would end up phoning **his** mum? It would have had to have been something pretty bad. Norm tried to rack his brains, but couldn't think what it might have been. Maybe it was something **else** that had upset Mikey? But again, Norm couldn't think what **that** could possibly be, either. Because as far as Norm could see, Mikey had it dead cushy. What had **he** got to worry about? Abso-flipping-lutely **nothing**.

"Norman?"

"Yeah?"

"What are you thinking?"

"Oh, you know," said Norm. "Just stuff."

"Stuff?" said Norm's mum.

Norm nodded.

"So you don't have any ideas, then?"

"About what?" said Norm.

"About why Mikey might be upset?"

"Oh, right," said Norm. "No, not really, Mum."

"Well, *I've* got one."

"One what?" said Norm.

"An idea."

Uh? thought Norm. If his *mum* had got an idea, why was she asking *him*, then?

"I think you should go and see him."

"What?" said Norm. "Oh, right. *That's* your idea? I thought you meant you'd got an idea why Mikey might be upset."

"That's what I want *you* to try and find out," said Norm's mum. "I want you to actually go and see him. Talk to him face to face. Not on Facebook."

146

"But..." began Norm.

"What, love?"

"I can't."

"What do you mean, you *can't?* Of course you can. He's your best friend!"

Norm shook his head. "I know. But I can't."

"Why not?"

"Dad's banned me."

Norm's mum pulled a face. "Dad's *banned* you from going to Mikey's?"

Norm nodded.

"What for?"

"For throwing out some aftershave."

"What?" said Norm's mum incredulously.

"Except I didn't."

Norm's mum didn't pull another face. There was no **need** to. She'd been pulling the **same** face for the last few seconds.

"Let me get this straight."

Good luck with **that**, thought Norm, who was still struggling to get his head round what had been going on that day.

"You've been banned from going to Mikey's for throwing out some aftershave?"

Norm nodded.

"Even though you didn't actually throw it out?"

Norm thought for a moment. "Pretty much, yeah."

"That's ridiculous."

"Tell me about it," said Norm.

"I'll have a word, love."

"With Dad?"

"Absolutely," said Norm's mum. "And in the meantime, you go and see your friend."

"But..."

"No buts, love. Just go."

"What? Now?"

Norm's mum nodded. "Don't worry. I'll take care of everything."

Norm didn't need telling twice. He was up and out the door before his mum could change her mind.

CHAPTER 11

Norm was in no mad rush to get to Mikey's. Or any other kind of rush, for that matter. Quite the opposite, in fact. For once in his life, Norm was perfectly content to dawdle along on his bike as if he had all the time in the world. He didn't care **how** many songs on his iPod it took. For a start he was just relieved to be out the house again. Happy to be free to go wherever he wanted. At least in theory, anyway. He wasn't actually going

to **go** wherever he wanted. He was going to go to Mikey's. But that wasn't the point. The point was he was free to go wherever he wanted if he **wanted** to.

Mainly, though, Norm was in no great hurry to get to Mikey's because he was in no great hurry to **talk** to Mikey. Well, he didn't mind **talking** to Mikey. He just didn't want to talk about why Mikey might be upset. Because that could only mean one thing. Mikey would inevitably start banging on all about his flipping **feelings** and stuff. And frankly Norm would sooner crawl across broken glass to smell one of John's farts than talk about flipping **feelings** and stuff. Mikey's feelings, or anybody **else's** feelings, for that matter. It was nothing personal.

On the other hand, thought Norm pedalling slowly through the woods, a friend in need is a friend indeed. Or was it the other way round? Was it a friend **indeed** is a friend in need? Who flipping cared? thought Norm. Either way there was only **one** thing for it. He was going to have to go and *see* Mikey. Talk to him in person. Face to face, as his mum had said. As opposed to Facebook to Facebook.

Eventually – and despite Norm's best efforts to put it off even *longer* – Norm *did* reach Mikey's street. But even then he slowed down to the point where if he'd been going any *slower* he'd have been going *backwards*.

Norm noticed Mikey way before Mikey noticed Norm. And the first thing Norm noticed – apart from Mikey himself – was the fact that Mikey didn't have some incredibly irritating girl poking her head over the fence, saying his name in a really annoying way and generally bugging the heck out of him, like a persistent bluebottle. As if Mikey didn't have it easy enough already, what with living in a nice big house and having a mother who made the world's greatest hot chocolate.

The second thing that Norm noticed – apart from Mikey himself – was the fact that Mikey's bike was in bits on the drive. A *lot* of bits. More bits, in fact, than Norm thought it was possible for a bike to actually be in.

"Whoa," said Norm not so much **skidding** to a halt on his bike as braking gently to a halt and putting his feet on the ground before he wobbled and fell off.

"Oh, hi, Norm," said Mikey looking up from the pile of bits.

"What's happening?" said Norm.

"What?" said Mikey.

"I said what's happening?" said Norm. "But it looks like it's already happened."

"Uh?" said Mikey. "Oh right. Yeah, I see what you mean."

Norm looked more closely at the bits of bike on the ground.

"Why did you take the pedals off?"

"What?" said Mikey absentmindedly.

"Why did you take the pedals off?" said Norm. "And the handlebars? And the seat? I thought you were just supposed to be fixing the **brakes?**"

"I was," said Mikey. "I mean, I **am**."

"So..."

"I got a bit carried away."

Norm laughed. "You're not flipping **kidding!**"

"I just can't seem to concentrate at the moment," said Mikey. "Sorry, Norm."

Norm was confused.

"It's *your* bike, Mikey. You can do what you want with it."

"Yeah, I know."

"So why are *you* sorry?"

"Well, because it means we still can't go biking," said Mikey.

"Oh right, yeah," said Norm. "I hadn't thought of that."

Mikey looked puzzled. "I *presume* that's why you came round?"

"Erm...yeah, kind of."

"*Kind* of?"

"No, really, that's why I came round. Mikey. Why

else would I come round? To help decorate?"

"Decorate **what?**" said Mikey.

Norm shrugged. "I dunno. Anything you want! It was just a joke, Mikey. Gordon flipping Bennet!"

Mikey looked at Norm. "Are you **sure** that's why you came round?"

Norm sighed. "All right, all right. It wasn't."

"I **knew** it," said Mikey.

"How come?" said Norm.

"Because you're **rubbish** at lying, Norm. That's how come."

Norm wasn't quite sure how to take this. Because on the one hand it was never particularly nice to be told that you're rubbish at something. Even if it **was** something that was generally considered to be completely wrong, and that you weren't **supposed** to be very good at anyway, like lying. On the other hand it still annoyed Norm. He'd always thought he was a pretty good liar and that he could blag his way out of most situations and predicaments, if necessary. But now all of a sudden, he was being told he wasn't as good as he **thought** he was. Why had Mikey never said anything before? What kind of flipping best friend **was** he?

"Well?" said Mikey.

"What?" said Norm.

"What else did you come round for? Apart from to go biking?"

They looked at each other for a moment. Mikey was first to crack a smile, followed a nanosecond later by Norm.

"You were saying?" said Norm.

"I was?" said Mikey. "When?"

"Earlier on."

"When, earlier on?"

"Much earlier on," said Norm. "When I was round before?"

Mikey looked confused. He was clearly in need of a bit more prompting. Norm duly obliged.

"When I was here last time and your mum made hot chocolate. You were about to say something, but my dad phoned and I had to go home."

"Oh, *right!*" said Mikey as the penny finally dropped.

"So?" said Norm.

"So, what?" said Mikey.

"What were you about to say?"

Mikey pulled a face. "Is that what you *really* came round for, Norm? To hear the rest of that sentence?"

Norm nodded. Actually that was *exactly* what he'd come round for. It was like Mikey had been on pause for the past couple of hours. It was time to hit 'play' again.

Mikey sighed. "I'm just a bit…"

"What?" said Norm.

"A bit…"

"*What?*" said Norm, a hint of exasperation already beginning to creep into his voice.

"A bit…"

Gordon flipping Bennet, thought Norm. If Mikey didn't flipping hurry up and *tell* him what he was, he'd...he'd...he'd...

"Worried," said Mikey eventually, saving Norm the hassle of thinking what he'd do. Which was fine by Norm. At least he'd found out why Mikey was upset. He was worried. Sorted. Mission accomplished. He could go back home and tell his mum, now.

"Erm..." began Mikey, when it became obvious that Norm wasn't going to say anything.

"What?" said Norm.

"Aren't you going to ask me what I'm worried **about?**"

"Uh?" said Norm.

"You weren't, were you?" said Mikey.

"What?" said Norm. "No, course I was, Mikey! I was just..."

"You were just what?"

Norm hesitated.

160

"Wondering how to phrase the question."

Mikey shook his head. "You're doing it again, aren't you, Norm? Being rubbish at lying?"

Norm sighed. It was a fair cop. He was being rubbish at lying again.

"Sorry, Mikey."

"'S'okay."

"So what are you worried about, then?"

"You really want to know?" said Mikey.

Norm nodded. "I really want to know."

"Mum and Dad."

Norm pulled a face. "You mean, *your* mum and dad?"

"What?" said Mikey. "Of course I mean *my* mum

and dad! Why would I be worried about **your** mum and dad, Norm?"

Norm snorted. "How long have you got?"

"Not long," said Mikey.

"Uh?" said Norm.

"Dad's going to be back any minute."

"Where from?"

"His run," said Mikey.

"Right," said Norm.

"Or at least that's what he **said** he was doing."

Norm looked at Mikey for a few seconds. Why would his dad say he was going for a run, if he wasn't actually going to **go** for a run? What **else** would he be doing? What a weird thing to say. And not like Mikey at all. Maybe **that's** what Norm's mum had meant when she was going on about Mikey acting differently and not being himself and all that stuff.

"I heard them, Norm."

"Who?" said Norm.

"My mum and dad. Last night."

Gordon Flipping Bennet

thought Norm. Was this about to get gross? Because if so, he was out of here.

"They were..."

Mikey suddenly stopped and gazed off into the distance. Whatever it was that his parents had been doing seemed to have had a profound effect on him.

"What, Mikey?"

"Arguing," said Mikey.

"Arguing?"

Mikey nodded.

Norm puffed his cheeks out in relief. "Is that all?"

"What do you mean, is that *all*, Norm? My mum and dad *never* argue!"

"Really?" said Norm.

"Really," said Mikey emphatically.

"But…"

"What?"

"Your mum said *everybody* argues from time to time."

"Yeah, but she was just *saying* that to make you feel *better*, Norm!" said Mikey beginning to sound more and more distraught. "She didn't actually *mean* it!"

"But..."

"She *didn't*, Norm!" yelled Mikey. "End of!"

"Whoa! What's going on, here?" said a voice.

Norm swivelled round to see a very hot and sweaty-looking Mikey's dad, standing at the end of the drive and wearing what looked very much to Norm like running gear.

"Hi, Mikey's dad," said Norm.

"Hello, Norman," said Mikey's dad. "Hello, Mikey."

"Hi, Dad," mumbled Mikey sheepishly.

"Well?" said Mikey's dad. "Someone care to fill me in? Who didn't?"

"Er, just someone we know at school," said Norm exchanging a quick glance with Mikey.

"And what didn't she do?"

"Pardon?" said Norm.

"This *someone* at school?" said Mikey's dad. "What didn't she do?"

"Er, nothing," said Norm.

"Nothing?" said Mikey's dad.

"No. I mean, yeah," said Norm.

"She didn't do anything at all?"

"Just...this...thing," said Norm.

"Hmm, I see," said Mikey's dad.

"How was your *run*, Dad?" said Mikey.

"Good, thanks."

"Where did you go?"

"Oh, you know, just the usual."

Mikey looked at his dad for a moment. "And where's *that?*"

"Pardon?" said Mikey's dad.

"Where's the *usual*, Dad?" said Mikey.

Mikey's dad pulled a face. "Why do you want to know?"

Mikey shrugged. "Why not?"

"Because you're not *normally* interested, Mikey. That's why not."

"Yeah, well I am now, aren't I?" said Mikey.

Mikey's dad looked at Norm, as if he was hoping that Norm was somehow going to be able to magically enlighten him and explain what on **earth** had got into Mikey. But Norm hadn't got the faintest idea. It really was beginning to look like his best friend had been abducted by aliens and replaced by some kind of grumpy clone.

"Well, if you **must** know, I went through the woods, past the allotments, round the park a couple of times and then back again."

Well, obviously Mikey's dad had come **back** again, thought Norm. Otherwise he wouldn't be flipping here now, would he? Not unless **he'd** been abducted by aliens and replaced by a flipping clone as well. Maybe **Norm** was the only one round here who **hadn't** been abducted by flipping aliens! He wouldn't be in the least bit surprised. No one told him **anything!**

"Happy now?" said Mikey's dad.

"Oh, yeah," said Mikey. "I'm completely ecstatic."

"Do I detect a note of sarcasm, Michael?"

Mikey shrugged.

"What's wrong?" said his dad.

"Nothing," said Mikey, shrugging again.

"Well, if you want to talk, just let me know," said Mikey's dad, heading up the drive.

"Whatever," muttered Mikey under his breath.

"Erm, Mikey?" said Norm, once Mikey's dad had disappeared into the house.

"Yeah?"

"You *were* being sarcastic, weren't you?"

Mikey sighed. "What do *you* think?"

Norm thought.

"I think you **were** being sarcastic."

"No, **really?**" said Mikey.

"You're doing it again, aren't you?" said Norm.

"Doing what?"

"Being sarcastic."

They looked at each other for a moment.

"Sorry, Norm," said Mikey. "Again."

"'S'all right," said Norm.

"I don't know what's got into me."

"Me neither," said Norm.

Mikey pulled a face. "You don't know what's got into **you?**"

"What?" said Norm. "No. I don't know what's got

into **you**, Mikey, you doughnut!"

Mikey laughed. But it wasn't a natural laugh. It was a rather tired, rather forced kind of laugh. The laugh of someone who knew that he was probably **expected** to laugh. Not because he'd found something particularly funny, but because it seemed rude **not** to.

"Come on, Mikey."

"What?"

"Tell me what's up."

"I can't."

"Why not?" said Norm.

"You'll think I'm being weird."

"I already think you're **weird**, Mikey."

"Well, stupid, then."

"No I won't," said Norm.

"Really?" said Mikey uncertainly.

"Really,"

"'Kay," said Mikey.

Norm waited expectantly.

"Ready?"

Norm nodded.

"I think my mum and dad are splitting up," said Mikey.

Whoa, thought Norm. Had he heard correctly? Had Mikey *really* just said that he thought his parents were splitting up? That wasn't possible. Well, it was possible that that's what Mikey had actually *said*. But it *wasn't* possible that that's what was actually *happening*. There was more chance of Norm marrying Chelsea and living happily ever after surrounded by a bunch of mini Norms and mini flipping Chelseas than there was of Mikey's parents splitting up. And *that* was never *ever* going to flipping happen!

"Well?" said Mikey. "What do you think?"

Norm didn't know *what* to think. Or what to say. *So* he said nothing.

"You did *hear* me, didn't you, Norm? I said I think my mum and dad might be splitting up."

Norm nodded. So he *had* heard correctly.

"Well?"

"*Might* be splitting up? Or *are* splitting up?"

"What?" said Mikey.

"Well, first you said you thought they **were** and then you said you thought they **might** be."

Mikey sighed wearily. "All I know is I heard them arguing."

"Yeah, but what **about?**" said Norm.

"I'm not sure."

"You're not **sure?**" said Norm. "But you still think they might be splitting up?"

Mikey sighed again, if anything even more wearily than before. "Well, if you must know, I think it had something to do with cheese."

OK, thought Norm. This time he definitely **hadn't** heard correctly.

"Sorry, Mikey but did you say..."

"Cheese, yeah," said Mikey.

Norm actually had to stifle a laugh.

"See, I **told** you you'd think I was stupid, Norm."

"Yeah, I know, Mikey. But I mean, come on."

"What?" said Mikey. "You think it's funny that I might become an orphan?"

"Uh?" said Norm. "**Orphan?**"

"Not an orphan," said Mikey. "A single parent. An only child. Oh, you know what I mean."

"Yeah, but all because of **cheese?**"

"I think it was more to do with the actual **kind** of cheese."

Norm pulled a face. "You mean there's more than **one** kind of cheese?"

"Yeah, course there is," said Mikey.

"You mean like, own brand and...*not* own brand?"

"No," said Mikey. "I mean there's loads of actual different *types* of cheese."

This was news to Norm. Then again, Norm's idea of a balanced diet was a pizza in each hand.

"Dad came back from the shops with this really expensive goat's cheese."

Norm was horrified. "Uh? You can make cheese from *goats?*"

"From goat's *milk*," said Mikey. "Not from actual *goats*."

"Oh, right," said Norm. "Thank goodness for *that!*"

"Anyway that's not the point," said Mikey.

"The point *is* – it was really expensive. A bit *too* expensive, apparently."

Ah, so basically what it all boiled down to was *money* then, thought Norm. Well, he knew exactly what *that* felt like – and had done ever since his dad had got the flipping sack and they'd had to move. Although he couldn't imagine Mikey's mum and dad ever actually being *short* of money. Or short of *anything*, for that matter.

"Do you understand?" said Mikey.

"Oh, yeah, sure," said Norm. "I mean who *hasn't* had a major falling out over the price of cheese at one time or another? You should have said before, Mikey. It all makes *much* more sense *now*."

Mikey sighed. "Now *you're* being sarcastic, Norm."

"Yeah, well, you know," said Norm. "And by the way, you're welcome."

"Welcome?" said Mikey. "What for?"

"For me digging you out of a hole," said Norm.

"Uh?" said Mikey. "What hole?"

"The 'someone' at school 'not doing anything'?" said Norm making quote marks in the air with his fingers. "Your dad *totally* believed me."

But Mikey didn't reply.

"So I'm obviously not *that* bad at lying, am I?"

Mikey still didn't reply and was gazing into the distance again.

"Mikey?"

"What?" said Mikey suddenly snapping out of it. "Sorry, Norm. I was miles away."

Norm looked at his best friend. Whether or not Mikey was being ridiculous worrying about his parents arguing over flipping cheese was neither here nor there. What mattered was that Mikey was **worried**. And thinking about it, thought Norm, thinking about it, was an argument over flipping **cheese** any more ridiculous than having a complete fit over some prehistoric aftershave? Probably not.

"Talking about being miles away," said Norm turning his bike round. "Well – a couple of miles, anyway.".

"What?" said Mikey. "You're not **going**, are you, Norm?"

"I can't stay **forever**, Mikey," said Norm.

"I'm not asking you to stay forever, Norm. Just a bit longer, that's all."

"What?" said Norm. "No, obviously. I knew that's

what you meant. But I've still got to go. It'll be tea by the time I get back."

Mikey looked at Norm for a moment, disappointment etched all over his face. Not that Norm noticed. "Well, in that case don't let me stop you."

"'Kay," said Norm pedalling off. "See you, Mikey."

Mikey sighed. "Yeah. See you, Norm."

CHAPTER 12

The further away from Mikey's he pedalled, the worse Norm began to feel. It wouldn't have hurt to stay a *little* bit longer, would it? But it was too late now. And anyway, what if there was a grain of truth in what Mikey was saying? What if there was *more* than a grain of truth in what Mikey was saying? What if there were *lots* of grains of truth in what Mikey was saying? What if his mum and dad really *were* on the brink of splitting up as a direct result of a cheese-related difference of opinion? Bizarre as that particular scenario might be. And as unlikely as it might *seem*. But what if it was actually true?

What was Norm supposed to have done? What **could** he have done? Should he have stayed at Mikey's and tried to somehow reassure him? Should he have put his arm around Mikey's shoulder and told him to cheer up, or snap out of it? That things could only get better? Because if it had been the **other** way round, Norm would have abso-flipping-lutely **hated** that! There was **nothing** more annoying than being told to cheer up when you didn't flipping **feel** like cheering up. Well, apart from being blamed for something you hadn't done. And never having enough money to buy stuff. And about 983 **other** things. But apart from **that** there was nothing more annoying than being told to flipping cheer up when you didn't flipping **feel** like cheering up.

"Yoo-hoo!" called a voice.

Norm didn't need to look to know who the voice belonged to. There was only one person he knew who ever actually **said** 'yoo-hoo'. But Norm had been so deep in thought that he hadn't even noticed he was **passing** the allotments, let alone that Grandpa was standing outside his shed with a spade in one hand and a bunch of carrots in the other.

"Hi, Grandpa," said Norm slowing to a halt.

"Thought you were ignoring me, Norman."

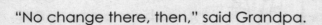

"What?" said Norm. "No. I just didn't know where I was."

"No change there, then," said Grandpa.

"Uh?" said Norm.

"You **never** know where you are."

"Very funny, Grandpa."

"You coming in, or what?"

Norm pulled a face. "Into the allotment, you mean?"

"No," said Grandpa. "Into a magical world full of snow queens, fairies and rainbows."

"Uh?"

"Of **course** I mean into the allotment, you great numpty."

Norm chuckled as he cycled round to the entrance of the allotments and let himself through the gate. If it had been anybody **else** taking the mickey out of him like that he'd have probably gone completely ballistic. Or at the very least got a bit cross. But it was just about **impossible** to be cross with **Grandpa**. Grandpa had the unerring ability to tickle Norm's funny bone even when Norm wasn't feeling particularly ticklish.

"In your own time, then," said Grandpa as Norm freewheeled up the path and got off his bike.

Norm pulled a face. "What?"

"I haven't got all day, you know."

"Really?" said Norm.

"Actually, you're right," said Grandpa. "I *have* got all day. What was I thinking?"

Norm laughed. It had been a weird day, to say the least. Coming to see Grandpa at the allotments had definitely been a good idea. Even if it hadn't actually been Norm's idea in the first place.

"Step into my office," said Grandpa.

"Office?" said Norm.

"All right, all right. Shed, then," said Grandpa. "There's a flask of tea and it's got your name on it."

Norm pulled another face. "How come it's got my name on it?"

"Good grief," said Grandpa

disappearing into the shed. "It hasn't **_literally_** got your name on it. It's just an expression."

"Oh, right," said Norm following.

"How do you take it?" said Grandpa as Norm stepped through the doorway.

"Take what?"

"Your tea."

"But..."

"What?" said Grandpa.

"I don't like tea," said Norm.

Grandpa frowned, his cloud-like eyebrows knitting together to form one **_big_** cloud.

"You don't like **_tea?_**"

"I like the kind of tea you

eat," said Norm. "Just not the sort of tea you *drink.*"

Grandpa sighed. "Well, you're no grandson of *mine*, then."

Norm laughed. "Good one, Grandpa."

"I'm not joking, Norman," said Grandpa unscrewing the top from a flask and pouring tea into a cup. "Until I see actual proof, I refuse to believe you and I are biologically related."

Norm looked at Grandpa for a moment before eventually Grandpa's eyes began to crinkle ever so slightly in the corners.

"Want to try some?"

"Nah, you're all right, thanks," said Norm, eyeing the brown liquid suspiciously.

"It won't kill you."

Possibly not, thought Norm. But by the looks of it, it could put him in hospital for a couple of weeks.

"So how come you were away with the fairies just now?" said Grandpa.

"How come I was **what?**" said Norm.

"Distracted," said Grandpa. "Not quite all there."

"I didn't say I wasn't quite all **there**, Grandpa. I just said I didn't know where I **was**."

"Whatever," said Grandpa.

"I was just…"

"What?"

"Thinking," said Norm.

"I've told you that's bad for you," said Grandpa.

Norm smiled.

"What were you thinking *about?*" said Grandpa. "And don't just say 'stuff'. Obviously you were thinking about *stuff*. What *kind* of stuff?"

Grandpa took a sip of tea and waited expectantly.

"Did you ever used to argue, Grandpa?"

"Argue?"

Norm nodded.

"You mean with your grandma?"

Norm nodded again. He'd never actually met Grandpa's wife. She'd died before he was born. He'd seen photographs, though. She looked a lot like Norm's mum. Which wasn't altogether surprising considering that she was Norm's mum's mum.

"All the time."

"What?" said Norm. "Really?"

"Well, not **all** the time," said Grandpa. "But sometimes. Yes, of course."

"About what?"

Grandpa shrugged. "All kinds of things."

"Like?" said Norm. "And don't just say 'stuff'."

Grandpa's eyes crinkled in the corners again. "I can't actually remember."

"Cheese?" said Norm.

"Pardon?" said Grandpa.

"Did you ever argue about cheese?"

"Cheese?"

"Yeah."

"What **kind** of cheese?"

Norm shrugged. "Dunno. Any kind of cheese."

Grandpa stroked his chin thoughtfully for a few seconds. "Not that I can recall, no. It was a long time ago now, Norman."

"Yeah, but..."

"What?" said Grandpa.

"You didn't..."

"Didn't what?" said Grandpa. "Come on, Norman. Spit it out."

"Split up," said Norm.

"Split up?" said Grandpa.

"Yeah."

"Because we argued sometimes?"

Norm nodded.

"No," said Grandpa. "Why do you ask?"

Should he say? wondered Norm. Should he actually tell Grandpa about Mikey being worried? Or would that be...what was the word? **Disloyal** of him? Perhaps he should try to change the subject? If it wasn't already too late. Which it might well be.

"Well?" said Grandpa.

Gordon flipping Bennet, thought Norm. It was too late.

"Nothing."

"What do you mean, **nothing?**" said Grandpa.

"I just wondered, that's all, Grandpa. No particular reason."

"Hmmm," said Grandpa as if he didn't totally believe Norm. Or even **partially** believe him. As if Norm might actually be lying. And not very well, either.

Norm had a sudden flash of inspiration. There was an unexpected opportunity here to change the subject if he wanted to. And at the same time do a little bit of detective work. Kill two birds with one stone, as it were. If that was the right expression? Not that Norm would ever actually contemplate killing two birds with one stone, of course. Or any birds, for that matter. Any more than he'd ever contemplate swinging a flipping *hamster* round his pathetic excuse for a garden.

"Er, Grandpa?"

"Yes?" said Grandpa pausing just as he was about to take another sip of tea.

"Have you seen Mikey's dad?"

"Mikey's **dad?**" said Grandpa. "Hmmm, let me see now."

Grandpa took the sip of tea and appeared lost in thought for a moment before eventually swallowing it.

"What does he look like?"

Norm sighed. What did Mikey's dad **look** like? He was **rubbish** at describing people. It would be different if he was describing a **bike**. He could describe a **bike** down to the last nut and bolt. But describing an actual **person?** That was different. So much for flipping **detective** work!

"Well?" said Grandpa.

"He's got a head," said Norm.

"Has he now?" said Grandpa. "Well, that's a start, I suppose."

Norm shrugged.

"Anything else?" said Grandpa. "Eyes? Ears?

Elbows?"

Norm nodded. "Yeah. All that stuff."

"Excellent," said Grandpa. "Well, we're really beginning to build up a picture here, Norman."

Yeah, thought Norm. A flipping **rubbish** picture.

"Does he look like Mikey?"

Hmmm, thought Norm. **Did** Mikey's dad look like Mikey? Actually, thinking about it, yes he did. Much older. Obviously. Be a bit weird if it was the other way round and Mikey looked older than his dad. But yes, essentially Mikey and his dad were like two beans in a tin. Or was it peas in a pod? Whatever, thought Norm. They looked like each other. That was the point.

"I suppose I **should** say does Mikey look like his dad," said Grandpa.

"Yeah," said Norm. "He does actually."

"In that case," said Grandpa, "I think I **have** seen him."

"You mean lately?" said Norm.

Grandpa regarded Norm curiously. "You didn't ask if I'd seen him **lately**. You just asked me if I'd *seen* him. As in, had I **ever** seen him."

thought Norm. Why couldn't everything be nice and straightforward? Why did it always have to be so flipping **complicated?** Like some kind of quiz or flipping word game. All he wanted to know was whether Grandpa had seen Mikey's dad and now all of a sudden he felt like he was being flipping irrigated! Or whatever that word was. Interrogated. That was it.

"As a matter of fact, I **have**," said Grandpa.

"What?" said Norm.

"I **have** seen him lately."

"Mikey's dad?"

Grandpa frowned. "That **is** who we're talking about, isn't it? Or are we talking about someone completely different now?"

"No, no," said Norm. "We're still talking about Mikey's dad."

"Excellent," said Grandpa. "I thought I was going round the bend for a minute!"

"When did you see him, Grandpa?"

"Oh, about half an hour ago."

"Really?"

"And then about twenty minutes ago."

"What?" said Norm.

"Well, first he ran past in one direction and then he ran back in the *other* direction."

Right, thought Norm. So that answered *that* question, then. Mikey's dad really *had* been for a run. Not that Norm ever thought that he *hadn't*. It was just Mikey who'd been all weird and suspicious about it.

"If that's who it was, of course," said Grandpa.

"No, sounds like it was, Grandpa."

"Why do you ask, Norman?"

Norm shrugged. "Just wondered."

"Hmmm, well that's odd."

"What is?"

"Well that's twice you've 'just wondered' something," said Grandpa. "First you wondered if your grandma and I ever argued about cheese and now you wonder if I've seen Mikey's dad."

"Yeah, well, you know," said Norm. "I'm just full of wonder."

"You're full of **_nonsense_**, Norman. That's what you're full of."

Norm smiled. There was nothing quite like a dose of Grandpa to cheer him up when he was feeling a bit down in the dumps. If he could bottle it and sell it he could make a flipping fortune! And it'd be a lot less smelly than Beast **_Pour_** flipping **_Homme!_**

"Seriously," said Grandpa

derailing Norm's train of thought. "What's going on? You know you can talk to me. I'm not going to blab."

Norm looked at Grandpa. He knew that was true. He **could** talk to him. And he knew that Grandpa would never **ever** blab.

"Mikey thinks his mum and dad are splitting up."

"I **knew** it!" said Grandpa triumphantly.

"Uh?" said Norm. "How come?"

"What?" said Grandpa. "No, I don't mean I knew Mikey's mum and dad were splitting up. I'm not psychic!"

"So…"

"I meant I knew you hadn't 'just wondered', that's all."

"Oh right," said Norm.

"So they've had an argument, have they?"

Norm nodded.

"About cheese?"

"Apparently."

"And according to Mikey that's that?" said Grandpa. "The end of the line? Game, set and match?"

"I know," said Norm. "What's he like, eh?"

"I mean it **could** be," said Grandpa.

"Really?" said Norm.

"Might just be the thin end of the wedge, Norman."

And what was **that** supposed to mean? thought Norm. Thin end of **what** flipping wedge? A wedge of cheese? What *was* it with flipping cheese today? Everyone was going cheese crazy!

"It might snowball into something much bigger,"

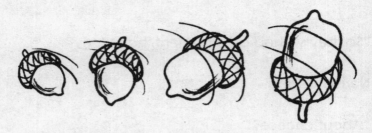

said Grandpa. "From small acorns and all that."

Norm pulled a face.

"Acorns?"

"From small acorns grow mighty oaks," said Grandpa. "Have you not heard that before?"

Not only had Norm not heard that before but he was beginning to think that it might be time to start heading home. He might as well. He could hardly understand a flipping word Grandpa was saying any more!

"It's probably nothing to worry about, though," said Grandpa. "Just a storm in a teacup."

"A what?" said Norm.

202

"Storm in a teacup."

"Is that a whatsit, Grandpa?"

"A whatsit?" said Grandpa. "What's a whatsit?"

Norm thought for a moment. "A thingyism?"

"You mean a **euphemism?**"

"Yeah, that's it," said Norm. "A **euphemism**. Like saying dropping the kids off at the pool when you mean having a..."

"No, it's just another expression," said Grandpa cutting Norm off.

"Right," said Norm.

"Tell Mikey worse things
happen at sea."

Gordon flipping Bennet, thought Norm. That was it. Enough was enough. He was off.

"Where are you going?" said Grandpa as Norm headed for the door.

"I've just remembered," said Norm stepping outside the shed and getting back on his bike. "I've got to see a man about a dog."

Norm hadn't got the faintest idea what *that* meant either. But under the circumstances that seemed only right.

CHAPTER 13

As Norm rode down his street for the second time that day, he spontaneously started to grin from one ear to the other. He just couldn't help it. He suddenly felt an overwhelming sense of joy. It was a very strange sensation. Well, for Norm it was, anyway. The only other time he'd felt even remotely like this was the time he'd discovered one final jammie dodger in the tin underneath all the boring digestives and rich tea biscuits. It was all he could do to stop himself from bursting into a spontaneous song and dance routine, as if he was in one of those stupid musicals his mum liked to watch. And

that hardly *ever* flipping happened. Actually, that had *never* flipping happened. And it wasn't because Norm was particularly overjoyed to see his stupid little house again either. Far from it. It was because he was overjoyed to see the sign sticking in the ground, in front of the house next *door* to his stupid little house.

FOR SALE.

That's all the sign said. Just two little words. But unlike some of the words Grandpa had just been coming out with, there was no mistaking what *they* meant. They meant freedom. Well, for Norm they did, anyway. Freedom from the world's most annoying occasional next door neighbour. Freedom from someone who never *ever* failed to make Norm want to pull his own hair out within two seconds of being in her company. Above all else, they meant freedom from someone who, for some reason, still thought it was highly amusing to **overemphasise** his name even though she'd already done it 150 billion times already. And that was **no** flipping exaggeration.

"Hello, **Norman!**" said Chelsea right on cue.

Gordon flipping Bennet, thought Norm. She was like one of those flipping meerkat things, popping up on the other side of the fence like that. She could have at least waited till he'd got off his flipping **bike** first.

"You don't look very happy to see me." Chelsea laughed.

"That's because I'm **not,**" mumbled Norm under his breath.

"Now, now, **Norman**. There's no need for **that**."

As far as Norm was concerned, though, there was **every** need for that. Whatever **that** flipping was.

Because as far as **Norm** was concerned he'd had just about enough of Chelsea and her snarky comments and her constant mickey-taking. Not to mention that flipping **laugh** of hers, which had the same effect on Norm as the sound of fingernails being scraped down one of those blackboard things from the olden days apparently had on other people.

But – and this really was a **huge** but – at least Norm wasn't going to have to put up with it for much longer. The laugh – or anything **else** about Chelsea, for that matter. Because Chelsea would soon be history. The kind of history that Norm actually **liked** – as opposed to all that boring stuff about kings and queens and whatever. But **how** soon? That's what Norm **really** wanted to know. Because if it was only going to be for a **little** while, then maybe

– just **maybe** – he could tolerate it. He could just bite his tongue and take a few deep breaths. Exactly how **many** deep breaths remained to be seen. Hopefully not **that** many, thought Norm opening the garage door and leaning his bike against the wall, where it belonged.

"Did you do the recycling?" said Chelsea.

Norm chose not to reply and instead took the first deep breath, before exhaling slowly and a little **too** noisily.

"You sound like you've got a puncture, **Norman!**"

"Uh?" said Norm checking his tyres by pressing them in turn with his thumb.

"Not your **bike**, silly," said Chelsea. "**You** sound like you've got a puncture!"

Norm could feel himself beginning to get more and more tense. This was clearly going to be **much** harder than he thought. But he **somehow** had to keep calm and carry on. Because if he didn't he was going to flipping well explode. And goodness knew what Chelsea would flipping say if *that* happened.

"Where are you going?" said Chelsea as Norm closed the garage and began heading towards the front door.

"Where does it flipping *look* like I'm going?" muttered Norm through gritted teeth.

"Language," said Chelsea.

Norm stopped and turned around. It was bad enough being told off by his little brothers for so-called *language*. But *Chelsea?* That just wasn't flipping on.

"What did you say?"

Chelsea smiled. "You know perfectly well what I just said. *Norman*."

Norm sighed.

"Is there a problem?"

"No," said Norm. "What makes you think that?"

Chelsea shrugged. "I don't know. You just seem a little..."

"A little what?" said Norm.

"Distant," said Chelsea.

Distant? thought Norm. He wasn't nearly as flipping distant as he'd *like* to be right now.

"And agitated."

"Agitated?"

Chelsea nodded.

"I don't know what you're talking about," said Norm.

"I think you know *exactly* what I'm talking about, **Norman**."

Gordon flipping Bennet, thought Norm. So now she knew what he was flipping **thinking**, did she? What was she? Some kind of **mind** reader? And anyway if she really *did* know what he was thinking, she wouldn't still be flipping **there!** She'd have gone the moment he'd arrived back home. In fact, thought Norm, if Chelsea really **did** know what he was thinking, she wouldn't have popped up over the fence in the first flipping place. She'd have stayed inside her own flipping house. Well, inside her **dad's** house, anyway.

"You know what I think?" said Chelsea.

Norm shrugged. Not only did he **not** know what Chelsea thought, he actually couldn't care **less** what Chelsea thought. Not unless she'd suddenly changed her mind and thought that everything she'd **ever** said or done to him was completely and utterly **wrong** and that she owed him an abso-flipping-lutely **massive** apology. But the odds of **that** happening, thought Norm, were slim, to say the least.

"I think that, deep down, you're a bit upset."

"Oh yeah?" said Norm.

"Yeah," said Chelsea. "I actually think you're going to miss me."

Norm stared at Chelsea in utter disbelief. "What?"

"I think you're actually going to miss me," said Chelsea. "In a **weird** kind of way."

A **weird** kind of way? thought Norm. If by that Chelsea meant the complete polar **opposite** of missing her then she was dead right. He would. But if she meant he was actually going to **miss** her, as in, you know, actually **miss** her, then she was off her flipping trolley! Did Chelsea even know what it **meant** to miss someone? Because it didn't flipping **look** like she did!

"I actually think you **like** our little chats," Chelsea went on. "I think you might even look **forward** to them."

Right, thought Norm. In the same way people in the olden days must have looked forward to going to the dentist and having all their teeth pulled out with a pair of rusty pliers and no anaesthetic apart from being whacked over the head with a flipping frying pan.

"And I'll tell you something else for nothing, **Norman**."

Oh goody, thought Norm. Because that was **just** what he flipping wanted. Chelsea to bang on even **more**.

"I think you like me, too."

Everything went very quiet. Norm stared at Chelsea. Had she **really** just said what he **thought** she'd just said?

"Well?" said Chelsea. "Aren't you going to say something?"

Norm opened his mouth, but no actual **sound** came out. Not only **that** but he could feel himself rapidly turning what he could only **assume** was the colour of a particularly overripe tomato. Either that or it had suddenly got very hot round here.

"You've gone red, **Norman**."

Norm sighed. He hardly needed Chelsea to tell him **that**. He **knew** he'd gone red.

"I mean **really** red."

Gordon flipping Bennet, thought Norm. He got the flipping picture. He'd gone red.

"We're talking visible from space red," said Chelsea.

Yes, thought Norm. And right now, space was precisely where he wished he flipping **was**.

"So it must be **true**, then?"

"What are you **talking** about?" squeaked Norm, finally regaining the power of speech but at the same time almost wishing that he hadn't. Because what was the **point?** It didn't matter **what** he said. She was just going to go on and on and flipping **on** about it. Like it was her mission in life to humiliate him at every opportunity. Which, for all Norm knew, it probably flipping was.

"You **know** what I'm talking about," said Chelsea.

Norm took another huge lungful of air before letting it slowly out again.

Chelsea suddenly burst out laughing.

"What?" said Norm.

"I'm only teasing, **Norman!**"

"Honestly?"

"Of course! Why would you like **me?**"

It was a good question, actually, thought Norm. Why **would** he like Chelsea? Why would **anybody** like Chelsea?

"I mean, it's not like I'm intelligent, funny **and** drop dead gorgeous, is it?" said Chelsea. "Oh no, wait. My mistake. I **am**."

Norm glared at Chelsea. She'd done it again. She'd dangled the bait and he'd fallen for it. Hook, line and flipping sinker!

"Seriously, though," said Chelsea, "I know we haven't **always** seen eye to eye."

Uh? thought Norm. They hadn't **always** seen eye to eye? They'd **never** seen eye to eye – and **wouldn't** ever see eye to eye if they lived next door to each other for the next 300 years! Which, luckily, **wasn't** going to happen now, what with her moving.

"But I just wanted to say..."

"What?" said Norm.

Chelsea sighed. "I just wanted to say that....well, it would be a shame for us to part on bad terms."

Norm thought for a moment. **Would** it? What was so wrong with parting on bad terms? They'd never **ever** been on remotely **good** terms in the first flipping place. So why break the habit of a lifetime? It wasn't like they were ever actually going to see each other again.
Well, **hopefully**
not, anyway.
It wasn't like
they were
going
to be

meeting up in years to come and laughing and joking and reminiscing about old times. Not if **Norm** could help it they weren't, anyway.

"Well?" said Chelsea.

"Well what?" said Norm.

All of sudden Chelsea didn't seem quite as sure of herself as usual. She seemed slightly hesitant and uncertain. Not that Norm noticed. "It's your turn to say something, Norman."

"Is it?" said Norm even failing to notice that possibly for the first time **ever** Chelsea had actually said his name quite normally, **without** overemphasising it.

"You know what?" said Chelsea.

Norm shrugged. "No, what?"

"Forget it," said Chelsea disappearing from **her** side of the fence, leaving Norm on **his** and wondering what exactly it was that he was supposed to forget. Because as far as Norm was concerned, he already had.

CHAPTER 14

"What's for tea, Mum?" said Norm as he walked into the kitchen and plonked himself down at the table.

"Hello, love, I'm fine, thanks for asking," said Norm's mum, standing stirring something at the cooker and without bothering to turn around.

"No, seriously, Mum," said Norm. "What's for tea?"

"Risotto."

Re-**whatto?** thought Norm.

"And some manners would be nice."

Some proper food would be even *nicer*, thought Norm.

"Well, Norman?"

"Sorry," said Norm. "I mean thank you. I mean please."

"That's better."

"Why can't we have pizza?"

"Are you *serious?*" said Norm's mum.

Was he *serious?* thought Norm. Course he was flipping serious. There were some things you *never* joked about. And pizza was one of them. How long had his mum known him?

"We had pizza for *lunch*, remember?" said Norm's mum.

Yeah, so? thought Norm. What exactly was his mum's point? If she even **had** one.

"Also, this isn't a restaurant."

Norm pulled a face. "Yeah, I know."

"So there's no menu."

Norm pulled another face. Or strictly speaking, continued pulling the **same** face as before. "Yeah, I know that too."

"So, in other words, there's no choice," said Norm's mum. "You get what you're **given**."

"Oh, right, I see," said Norm. "Fair enough."

Norm's mum laughed. "Yes, it **is** fair enough actually, Norman."

Norm's mum continued to stir for several seconds before curiosity finally got the better of her.

"Well?"

"Well what?" said Norm.

"*Pardon?*"

"Sorry," said Norm. "I mean well what, *please?*"

"How did you get on?"

Norm thought for a moment. How did he get on *where?* And doing *what?* There'd been a lot going on lately..

"At Mikey's?" prompted Norm's mum. "Trying to find out why he might be upset?"

"Oh, right, that," said Norm..

"Don't tell me you've *forgotten!*"

OK, thought Norm. He wouldn't.

"That was the whole point of you **going**, love!"

"Going where?" said a voice.

Norm swivelled round to see his dad standing framed in the kitchen doorway like a painting. Not that Norm could imagine anyone ever wanting to paint his **dad**.

"Well, Norman? I'm waiting."

"Erm..." began Norm.

"He's been to Mikey's," said Norm's mum, finally turning around.

"Pardon?" said Norm's dad, the vein on the side of his head already beginning to throb. Not that Norm noticed.

"I **said** he's been to Mikey's."

"But..."

"What?" said Norm's mum.

"He's **banned!**" said Norm's dad as if he couldn't quite believe what he was hearing.

"Banned from what?"

"Going to Mikey's."

"Banned from going to Mikey's?" said Norm's mum.

Norm's dad nodded.

Norm's mum pulled a face. "That's a bit harsh, isn't it?"

"You reckon?"

"Er, yes I *do* reckon, actually," said Norm's mum.

Norm was starting to feel like he was watching a tennis match, turning his head from side to side, faster and faster as his mum and dad traded shots. Not that

Norm had ever actually **been** to a tennis match before. Or even **liked** tennis.

"You don't know what he did," said Norm's dad.

"Actually I **do** know what he did," said his mum. "Or at least I know what you **think** he did. You think he threw out some stupid old aftershave."

The silence in the kitchen was almost deafening. But it didn't last for long.

"Some stupid old aftershave?" said Norm's dad.

Norm's mum nodded.

"Some **stupid** old aftershave?"

Norm's mum nodded again.

"**Stupid?**" said his dad.

Norm was beginning to wonder whether he should butt in. Because this conversation was clearly going nowhere fast. Was this **really** what happened when you got old? You ended up arguing about flipping **aftershave?** And **cheese?** It was like some nightmarish vision of the future.

"Beast **Pour Homme?**" said Norm's dad.

Norm's mum shrugged.

"You don't remember?"

Norm looked at his mum. Whatever it was that she was supposed to remember, she'd obviously forgotten.

"Well, **that's** nice," said Norm's dad.

"What is?" said Norm's mum.

Yeah, thought Norm. What is? Whatever it was he wished his dad would hurry up and flipping **tell** them.

"Oh, wait a minute," said Norm's mum.

Norm sighed. Did they really **have** to?

"Is that the stuff you had on..."

"For our first date?" said Norm's dad interjecting. "Yes, as a matter of fact it is. Or was, anyway."

"I **see!**" said Norm's mum. "So **that's** why you made such a big fuss about it!"

Norm's dad nodded sheepishly.

"I didn't know you were so sentimental."

"Yeah, well, you know."

Norm's mum smiled. "Aw, come here."

No, please **don't**, thought Norm as soon as he realised what was happening. But it was too late. His dad had already crossed the kitchen and had been enveloped in an octopus-like embrace by his mum.

"Silly sausage," said Norm's mum ruffling his dad's hair before planting a big juicy kiss smack on his lips.

Gordon flipping Bennet, thought Norm. Had he suddenly become invisible or something? His parents *did* actually know he was still **there**, didn't they? Perhaps they thought he'd gone. He certainly wished he flipping **had** gone. Because this was one of the most disgusting things he'd ever had the misfortune to witness in his entire life. Should he say something? Then again what **could** he say? Apart from, "Please stop, I'm going to be sick"?

"Aw, yuk!" said Dave appearing in the doorway.

"They're just **kissing**, Dave!" said Brian appearing beside him. "It's perfectly **natural**."

Yeah, thought Norm. So was going to the toilet. Didn't mean you had to do it in flipping **public**, though, did it?

"Hello, boys," said Norm's mum finally untangling herself from his dad. "Ready for some tea?"

"Yes, Mum," said Norm's brothers simultaneously.

"You'd better wash your hands, then."

"You'd better wash **yours**," muttered Norm.

"What was that, love?" said Norm's mum.

"Nothing, Mum," said Norm as the dog wandered into the kitchen and headed straight for his bowl in the corner.

Norm's dad looked at John and pulled a face. "Is it raining outside?"

What? thought Norm. As opposed to raining **inside?**

"Don't think so," said Dave. "Why?"

"What's happened to all John's curls?"

"We straightened them," said Brian.

"You **straightened** them?" said Norm's dad incredulously..

Norm's mum sniffed. "Never mind that. What's that smell?" She sniffed again. "It's absolutely revolting. But at the same time strangely familiar."

Norm and Dave exchanged a quick glance. Not only that, but Norm's mum *saw* Norm and Dave exchange a quick glance. Not that Norm **noticed** his mum noticing him and Dave exchange a quick glance. He was too busy wondering whether Dave would take this opportunity to confess his role in The Great Aftershave Mystery – as it would no doubt be called if this was some stupid book – and at the same time help to clear Norm's name.

"I'd better go and wash my hands, then," said

Dave, disappearing towards the stairs.

Norm sighed. Well, that answered **that** flipping question then, didn't it? How could he have been so **stupid?** Did he honestly think that Dave would admit it just like that? What on earth had he been thinking? And there was no point Norm protesting his innocence and grassing Dave up himself. Who was his dad going to believe? Him or his stupid little brother? No, his dad had obviously made his mind up and **nothing** was going to change it. Norm was guilty. Same as flipping always.

CHAPTER 15

Sunday morning dawned bright and clear. Which was excellent news as far as Norm was concerned because it meant that he could go biking. Not that there was ever any doubt that Norm was going to go biking. If he'd woken up to find Grandpa's shed had blown into the back garden or the house floating down the street, he would have *still* gone biking. He'd made his mind up the night before, when Mikey had messaged him on Facebook to say that he'd managed to fix his brakes. They were officially 'good to go'. And *go* was precisely what Norm intended to do. He didn't care where. As long as they went **somewhere**. And the fact that it was a lovely day was the icing on the cake. Or, as Norm preferred to think of it, the extra cheese topping on a twelve inch deep crust margherita pizza from Wikipizza.

For once, all was well in Norm's world as he pedalled down the street. **Relatively** well, anyway. About as well as could be expected. Not that Norm's expectations were ever all that great. But at least he'd been allowed out. Officially allowed out, that was. He hadn't had to **sneak** out without his dad knowing. The so-called **ban** had been lifted, once his mum had explained to his dad why Norm had gone over to see Mikey in the first place. And once Norm had told his mum and dad why Mikey had been **upset** in the first place. Of course, they'd said pretty much the same as Grandpa had said. That there was probably nothing at all for Mikey to worry about. That just about everybody argued **sometimes**. Except that they'd managed to say it without going on about acorns and oak trees and flipping storms in eggcups or whatever.

Norm gave an involuntary shudder as he suddenly recalled the horrifying moment when his mum had kissed his dad. It was an image that would haunt him forever. The kind of image that once **seen** could never ever be **unseen**. Not only that, thought Norm, but it had also been completely out of order. His mum and dad were nearly flipping **forty** for goodness sake. It should be **illegal** to kiss at that age. It was like something you saw on the flipping Discovery Channel. Except even **more** gross. Not that his dad seemed to mind. Quite the opposite, in fact. His dad had been in a surprisingly good mood for the rest of the evening. And the last Norm had seen of his mum she'd been looking at aftershave on one the shopping channels.

If Norm had been more focused, and concentrating on riding his bike rather than dwelling on the night before, he might have seen the car earlier. And if Norm had seen the car earlier he might not have had to swerve and skid to avoid hitting it. If Norm hadn't had to swerve and skid to avoid hitting it he might not have noticed that sitting in the driver's seat was none other than Mikey's mum. And that sitting **next** to Mikey's mum in the **passenger** seat was none other than some completely random bloke who Norm had never clapped eyes on before in his life.

Of course it was all ifs and buts. Because Norm **wasn't** completely focused on riding his bike. He **did** have to swerve and skid to avoid hitting the car. And he **did** notice that Mikey's mum was sitting in the driver's seat. Except luckily, the car was actually parked at the side of the road at the time. So it could have been a lot worse, thought Norm, as he regained his composure and carried on down the road towards Mikey's house as if nothing had happened. Except that something

had just happened. Something that Norm really, **really** wished **hadn't** just happened. And not the almost crashing bit, either. Norm was always nearly crashing. Well, not **always** nearly crashing. But he quite often nearly crashed. And sometimes he actually **did** crash. It was all part and parcel of mountain biking. How on earth was Norm ever going to become World Champion if he didn't learn how to take the rough with the smooth? If he didn't accept that from time to time he was going to fall off or come off second best in a collision with a tree, then he might as well take up embroidery for a hobby instead.

No, the thing that Norm **really** wished hadn't just happened was seeing Mikey's mum sitting in the car with a total stranger next to her, as he whizzed past. Well, a stranger to Norm, anyway. By the looks of things the man wasn't a stranger to Mikey's mum, because as far as Norm could tell, he'd just said something that had made her laugh.

But Norm was pretty sure she hadn't seen him. At least if she **had**, she hadn't **acknowledged** him. Which was probably a good thing. Because that could have been very embarrassing. And pretty awkward too, thinking about it, thought Norm.

The problem was – should Norm say something to Mikey or not? Well, obviously he was going to have to say **something** to Mikey. He wasn't just going to turn up on his doorstep and then not speak. That would be rude. And, to be honest, pretty weird as well. But should he say something to Mikey about what he'd just **seen?** About what he'd just stumbled upon? About what he'd just **witnessed?** That was the problem. Because what with Mikey being convinced his mum and dad were on the verge of splitting up, that was probably the **last** thing he wanted to hear. Or **needed** to hear. And actually, thought Norm, it was beginning to look like Mikey could well be right after all. Perhaps he **wasn't** putting two and two together and getting twenty two. Perhaps he **wasn't** making a mountain out of a flipping acorn, or whatever that expression was. Perhaps there really **was** a grain of truth in what Mikey had said the day before.

If Norm had been more focused and concentrating on riding his bike, he might have seen Mikey a bit earlier. And if Norm had seen Mikey a bit earlier he might not have had to swerve and skid to avoid hitting him as he turned out of his drive. But once again, it was all ifs and buts.

"Whoa! Mind where you're going, Norm!" shrieked Mikey, wobbling and very nearly riding straight into a lamppost.

Gordon flipping Bennet, thought Norm who hadn't even realised he was anywhere **near** Mikey's street, let alone that Mikey was actually cycling **along** it.

"You could at least apologise," said Mikey.

"Sorry, Mikey," said Norm.

"It's all right," said Mikey. "It's one way of testing the brakes, I suppose."

They looked at each other for a few seconds before Mikey eventually smiled. But Norm remained stony-faced.

"What's up?"

Norm shrugged. "Nothing much."

"Something is," said Mikey. "I can tell."

"How?"

"Ah, so there *is* something up, then?"

"What?" said Norm. "No there isn't. I didn't say that."

"Come on, Norm," said Mikey. "You can tell *me*."

Norm sighed. Mikey was right. He *could* tell him. But he still didn't know whether he *should* tell him.

"What *is* it?" said Mikey.

Norm sighed again. "I can't say."

"*Can't* say? Or *won't* say?"

It was a good question, thought Norm. If only he could think of a half decent answer.

"Well?" said Mikey who clearly wasn't giving up until he'd got to the bottom of whatever it was that Norm either couldn't, or wouldn't say.

"How's your mum?"

Mikey pulled a face. "Pardon?"

"How's your mum?" said Norm. "And your dad?"

"That's a bit random, isn't it, Norm?"

Norm shrugged. "Maybe."

"I see," said Mikey. "So *that's* what this is about, is it? My mum and dad?"

"Maybe," said Norm again.

"Is that all you're going to say? Maybe?"

Norm looked at Mikey. "Maybe."

There was an awkward pause. A plane flew overhead while, in the distance, a clock struck ten. Not that Norm noticed. For all Norm knew, a clock could have flown overhead and a plane struck ten.

"Do you know something?" said Mikey after a while.

"What?" said Norm expectantly.

"Uh?" said Mikey. "No, Norm. I mean, do **you** know something?"

"Oh, right," said Norm eventually twigging what Mikey meant. "Erm, maybe."

Mikey sighed. "Stop saying **maybe**, Norm! Do you know something or not?"

They looked at each other for a few moments before Norm gave a slight nod.

"Well?" said Mikey getting more and more exasperated. "**What** do you know?"

"I think I just saw your mum," mumbled Norm staring at the ground.

"You **think** you just saw my mum?"

"I *did* just see your mum."

"**Where?**"

"In a car."

Mikey looked puzzled. "A car? But..."

They both turned to look at Mikey's dad's car, parked on the drive behind them.

"There was..." began Norm.

"There was **what?**" said Mikey.

Norm sighed. "A man with her."

"A man?" said Mikey. "In the **same** car?"

Norm resisted his natural urge to say something sarcastic. For once in his life he didn't even **think** anything sarcastic. This was **much** too important. Or at least it might be.

"What were they doing?" said Mikey.

"Talking," said Norm.

"Talking?"

"And laughing."

"*Laughing?*"

Norm nodded.

"But…" began Mikey.

"I know what you're thinking, Mikey," said Norm despite the fact that he hated it when other people said that to *him*.

"Do you, Norm?" said Mikey. "Do you *really?*"

"Erm, well I think I do, anyway," said Norm hesitantly. "I think you're thinking…"

"I *know* what you think I'm thinking!" said Mikey.

Gordon flipping Bennet, thought Norm. So if Mikey *knew* what he thought he was thinking, why did he flipping *ask?*

"You think I'm thinking that that just goes to **prove** it!" said Mikey. "That what I said yesterday must be true!"

"Erm...maybe," said Norm.

"I **told** you, Norm!" wailed Mikey. "And stop saying **maybe!**"

"Hi, guys," said a voice.

Norm spun around to see Mikey's dad coming out the front door, dressed in his running gear.

"Hi, Dad," said Mikey.

"Hi, Mikey's dad," said Norm.

"**What** did he tell you, Norman?" said Mikey's dad doing a few stretches.

"Sorry?" said Norm knowing perfectly well what Mikey's dad was referring to, but stalling for time while he thought of something to say.

"What did Mikey tell you?"

Norm and Mikey exchanged a quick glance.

"Erm, nothing," said Norm.

"Nothing?" said Mikey's dad who by now had begun jogging on the spot.

"Just something about a girl," said Norm who by now had begun wishing that Mikey's dad would flipping hurry up and go on his flipping run.

"A **girl**, eh?" Mikey's dad grinned. "The same one?"

"Pardon?" said Norm.

"The same girl you were talking about **yesterday?**"

Norm stared blankly at Mikey's dad. He had no idea what he was talking about.

"You know, Norm?" said Mikey staring wide-eyed

at his friend. "The **someone** we know at school?
The one who didn't do anything?"

"Oh **right!**" said Norm finally remembering. "Yeah.
I mean no. A different one."

"A **different** girl, eh?" said Mikey's dad. "I won't
ask!"

Good, thought Norm. Because why on earth had
he said **that?** All he was doing was trying to help
Mikey out of a sticky situation and
to stop his dad from rumbling
what they were **really** talking
about. And now he was
completely out of his depth.
Any **further** out of his depth
and he was going to
need flipping diving
gear! It would be **so**
much easier to just tell
the truth sometimes.

"Hadn't you better get off
on your run, Dad?" said
Mikey.

"Are you trying to get rid of me, Mikey?" Mikey's dad laughed.

"No!" said Mikey. "What makes you think *that?*"

"Anyway, you're right. I *should* get off. Your mum'll be back soon."

Norm and Mikey exchanged another glance. Only this time not quite so quick.

"What is it?" said Mikey's dad.

"Nothing, Dad," said Mikey. "Back from where?"

"Sorry, what?"

"You said Mum'll be back soon."

"That's right," said Mikey's dad.

Mikey hesitated. "Back from where?"

"Where?"

"Yeah," said Mikey. "Where is she?"

Mikey's dad pulled a face. "Didn't she tell you?"

Mikey shook his head.

"I thought you knew."

Gordon flipping Bennet, thought Norm. Knew **what?** Why couldn't Mikey's dad just come out and flipping **say** it? And it wasn't even **his** mum they were talking about here. So whatever **he** was feeling, **Mikey** must be feeling a **million** times worse!

"Your mum's learning to drive."

Everything suddenly went very quiet as Norm and Mikey digested what Mikey's dad had just said. Somewhere in the distance a car horn tooted and a dog barked. Not that Norm noticed. For all Norm knew, a car could have barked and a dog tooted.

"So..." began Mikey.

Mikey's dad nodded. "She's having her first driving lesson, yes."

"Right," said Mikey.

"Right," said Norm.

"And did she tell you about the holiday?"

"Holiday?" said Mikey. "What holiday?"

"The one we're going to book? This afternoon?"

Norm pulled a face. "You're going on holiday this afternoon?"

"No, Norman!" laughed Mikey's dad. "We're not **going** on holiday this afternoon. We're **booking** a holiday this afternoon! Or at least we're hoping to."

"Right," said Norm.

"Right," said Mikey.

"Which is why I really **do** have to get a move on!"

said Mikey's dad setting off. "See you later, guys!"

"See you, Mikey's dad," said Norm.

"Yeah, see you, Dad," said Mikey.

They watched as Mikey's dad gradually got smaller and smaller before finally disappearing round the corner.

"So," said Norm.

"So," said Mikey.

"Driving lesson, eh?" said Norm.

"Yep," said Mikey.

"And a holiday?"

Mikey nodded.

"Doesn't look like they're planning on splitting up anytime soon, then?" said Norm.

"Doesn't, does it?" said Mikey.

They looked at each other for a moment.

"Happy now?" said Norm.

"Happy now," said Mikey.

"Excellent," said Norm. "In that case, let's go."

"Uh?" said Mikey. "Go where?"

"On a flipping bike ride, you doughnut!" yelled Norm pedalling off down the road.

CHAPTER 16

It was only after Norm and Mikey had had their bike ride and gone their separate ways again that Norm was able to reflect on what a topsy-turvy couple of days it had been. Talk about a flipping emotional rollercoaster. In fact, the last couple of days made an emotional rollercoaster seem like one of those roundabouts at fairgrounds where little kids got to sit in a car, a fire engine, or, if they were feeling particularly adventurous, on the top of a tiny double decker bus.

But at least Mikey was happy now. That was the main thing. Even if he **was** a complete and utter jammy doughnut. A **holiday?** Some people had **all** the flipping luck, thought Norm as he zoomed through the woods, heading for home. Because the only holiday **he'd** be going on anytime soon would be a flipping supermarket own brand holiday. Unless his dad hurried up and got a flipping job, of course. And there didn't seem much chance of **that** happening.

Despite everything, though, Norm couldn't help smiling to himself. It hadn't been funny at the time, of course, but looking back, it was actually pretty hilarious. Seeing Mikey's mum in the car with that guy who turned out to be her driving instructor? You couldn't make it up, thought Norm. Although, thinking about it now, that was kind of what he had done. No harm done, though. Luckily.

All in all, then, thought Norm as he screeched round the corner into his own street, it was shaping up to be a half decent day. Or a half **rubbish** one, depending on which way you looked at it. But if there was any last, lingering doubt which way **Norm** was going to look at it, that doubt was about to get smashed into a thousand tiny pieces.

It wasn't as if Norm had **forgotten** about the 'For Sale' sign sticking in the ground outside Chelsea's dad's house. How **could** he forget about something so monumentally, earth-shatteringly, life-changingly important as **that?** That would be like forgetting how to sleep. Or, in Norm's case, forgetting how to eat **pizza**. So the sign **itself** didn't take Norm by surprise. What took Norm by **surprise** was the sticker that had been plastered **onto** the sign. Over those two little but oh so **beautiful** words. This time, however, it was just **one** little four letter word. A word which not only took Norm's breath away, very nearly blew his socks off as well.

Norm skidded to a halt at the end of his drive and stared at the sign for a few seconds, scarcely able to believe his eyes. It had happened. It had actually flipping *happened*. And an awful lot sooner than Norm could have possibly *ever* hoped. Or wished. Or dreamed. Because that's what this was, thought Norm. A dream come flipping true. He quite literally could *not* be happier. Nothing – abso-flipping-lutely *nothing* – was going to spoil *this* moment. Even Chelsea popping up on the other side of the fence, as she inevitably would.

"Hello, *Norman!*" said Chelsea popping up on the other side of the fence.

"Hi," said Norm cheerily.

"Ooh!" said Chelsea. "*Someone's* in a good mood!"

"Yeah, well, you know."

Chelsea tilted her head and smiled. "Any particular reason?"

"What?"

"Any particular *reason* for being in a good mood?"

Norm shrugged. "Not really."

"Funny," said Chelsea.

"Is it?" said Norm.

"Well, let's face it, **_Norman_**, you're never exactly a **_bundle_** of laughs, are you?"

"Really?" said Norm.

"You're normally all snarky and sarky and grouchy and grumpy."

"Thanks," said Norm.

"No offence."

"None taken."

"And you weren't very nice to me last night."

"I wasn't?"

"When I was upset."

Norm thought for a moment. "You were upset?"

"Yes I **was**, actually," said Chelsea. "But I'm feeling much better now, thanks for asking."

Norm pulled a face. "I **didn't**."

"Exactly!" said Chelsea.

Norm sighed. He had even **less** of an idea than usual what Chelsea was on about. And **that** was flipping saying something.

"So anyway I was just wondering if..." Chelsea left the end of the sentence hanging in mid-air. Norm knew **exactly** what she was just wondering. She was wondering if the reason Norm suddenly seemed so cheerful and full of the joys of spring was because he'd seen the sign. Of course, that was **precisely** the reason he was suddenly so cheerful and full of the joys of spring! But there was no flipping **way** he was going give **her** the satisfaction of hearing him actually say that. Why **should** he give her the satisfaction of hearing him say it? After all the grief and aggravation **she'd** caused **him?** No way, thought Norm. She could wonder all she flipping wanted, as far as he was concerned.

"What?" said Norm.

"Don't tell me you haven't **noticed**," said Chelsea.

"Noticed what?" said Norm innocently.

"The sign?"

Norm looked
up at the sign.
"Oh, right.
see."

"Seriously?"
said   Chelsea.
"You   hadn't
noticed?"

Norm shrugged. "Nah."

"You know something?" Chelsea laughed.

"What?" said Norm.

"You're rubbish at lying!"

Norm **thought** about arguing. But didn't. He just couldn't be bothered any more. And anyway, she'd soon be gone. Forever.

"So what are you thinking, **Norman?**"

"I, er..." began Norm.

"Actually, it's OK. I **know** what you're thinking."

Did she? wondered Norm. Did she **really** know what he was thinking? Because he'd be pretty impressed if she **did**.

"You're thinking that on one hand this is the best news **ever**," said Chelsea. "But on the other hand you're **also** thinking that you don't want me to **know** that you're thinking that this is the best news ever."

Whoa, thought Norm. She was **good**. She was **really** good.

"So it's OK," said Chelsea.

"What is?" said Norm.

"You don't have to pretend to be sad."

"I'm not," said Norm.

Chelsea smiled. "You're not **pretending**, or you're not **sad?**"

Norm pulled a face. The truth was he really wasn't sure **what** he was thinking any more.

"Anyway, there's no **need** to be sad, **Norman**," said Chelsea.

"What do you mean?" said Norm.

"I'm not going anywhere."

Norm **heard** the words. He just didn't know what to **make** of them.

"You'll never guess who's bought the house." Chelsea grinned.

Norm sighed. She was right. He never would. So why didn't she just hurry up and flipping **tell** him?

"My mum."

"Uh?" said Norm. "Your **mum?**"

"That's right," said Chelsea. "My mum."

Norm looked at Chelsea for a moment. A moment that seemed to last an eternity but which in reality, only lasted for a couple of seconds. It was still plenty long enough, as far as Norm was concerned, though.

"So you know what *that* means, **Norman?**"

Norm nodded. He knew **exactly** what that meant. It meant that Chelsea wouldn't only be living next door to him at **weekends**. It meant she'd be living next door to him **all** the flipping time.

It meant the end of the flipping world, as Norm knew it.

"Isn't that **great?**" said Chelsea.

"What?" said Norm distractedly.

"I said isn't that great?" said Chelsea. "We're going to **proper** neighbours now!"

Gordon flipping Bennet, thought Norm.

CHAPTER 17

All Norm wanted to do was sneak up to his room and chill for a bit. Or at least **try** to chill for a bit, anyway. Drool over a few bikes on his iPad. Maybe watch some videos. Anything to take his mind off the pants-soiling **horror** of what he'd just discovered, if only temporarily. But oh no. He couldn't be allowed to just do **that**, could he? Because that would be **way** too much to ask!

"Is that you, Norman?" called his dad, before Norm had even had the chance to close the front door behind him.

Gordon flipping *Bennet*, thought Norm. What now? *Surely* things weren't about to get even *worse*, were they? How much worse could things actually *get?* Wasn't it bad enough that Chelsea was going to be living next door *permanently?* That was already the stuff of flipping *nightmares*, as far as *Norm* was concerned. He dreaded to think what *else* might be in store for him.

"We're in here, love!" called Norm's mum.

Norm sighed. "Where?"

"Front room!"

"'Kay," said Norm heading for the stairs. "See you later."

"Norman!" yelled Norm's dad.

"Yeah?"

"Get in here!"

Uh? thought Norm. Why didn't they just **say** that in the first flipping place, then? How was **he** supposed to know that his parents actually wanted to **see** him?

"Now!" yelled Norm's dad.

"All right, all right, keep your flipping hair on," muttered Norm under his breath, turning round.

"Nice of you to join us," said Norm's dad as Norm appeared in the doorway a moment later.

"Don't mention it," said Norm, failing to notice his dad's sarcasm. He was much more concerned by the fact that, sitting crammed between his mum and dad on the sofa, like sardines in a tin, were Brian and Dave. It looked like they'd all

been waiting for him. As if being summoned into The Front Room Of Doom wasn't ominous enough in itself. What was about to happen? wondered Norm. Because **something** was **definitely** about to happen. He hadn't just been called in to talk about the weather, or the price of flipping loft insulation. And apart from anything else, how come his dad had asked if it was him as he came in the front door? Everyone else was already **there!** Who did his dad **think** it was? The flipping **Gruffalo?**

"Sit down, love," said Norm's mum. "Dave's got something to say to you."

Norm did as he was told and sat down, in the armchair. Not that there was much choice. It was the only place **left** to sit. Almost as if it had been **deliberately** left for Norm to sit in. Like he was some kind of visiting VIP or guest of honour. Although Norm seriously doubted that he was about to be

treated like one.

Norm sat and waited. All eyes were on him. As if everyone expected ***him*** to say something and not the other way round.

"Go on then, Dave," said Brian giving his brother a dig in the ribs with his elbow.

"Ouch!" said Dave. "Brian just..."

"Never mind that," said Norm's mum. "What have you got to say to Norman?"

Yes, thought Norm. What ***had*** Dave got to say to him? The suspense was killing him.

"Sorry, Norman," said Dave.

Sorry? thought Norm. For what? He could think of about a ***million*** flipping things Dave should be ***sorry*** for. He was going to have to be a bit more specific than ***that***.

"About the aftershave."

Norm looked at Dave. Then at his mum and dad. Then back to Dave again. "You mean…"

Norm's mum nodded. "He's told us everything, love. With a *little* bit of persuasion. Isn't that right, Dave?"

Dave nodded sheepishly.

"I saw that look you two gave each other last night," said Norm's mum. "I just put two and two together. Call it maternal instinct."

Whoa, thought Norm. He didn't particularly care *what* his mum called it. This was brilliant. And not what he'd been expecting at all. But if *that* was a surprise, what happened *next* was practically a *miracle*.

"Sorry, son," said Norm's dad.

"Pardon?" said Norm as if his dad had just announced he'd been a dolphin in a previous life.

"I said I'm sorry. For blaming you. And for banning you from going to Mikey's. I shouldn't have assumed."

No, thought Norm. He flipping **shouldn't** have. But it had never stopped him in the past, had it?

"**And...?**" prompted Norm's mum, glancing across the sofa at his dad.

"Oh yeah," said Norm's dad as if he'd just remembered. "To make up..."

Now **this** was more like it, thought Norm. Not only was his dad **apologising**, but he was actually going to make up for it? How? By offering to buy him a new bike? By setting up his own personal account at Wikipizza? Just giving him some money? Because as far as Norm was concerned, all three options would be perfectly acceptable.

"Go on," said Norm's mum encouragingly.

"I'd like to give you this," said Norm's dad, producing an all-too-familiar-looking, small, square-shaped glass bottle from behind his back.

Norm couldn't believe it. All that flipping build up? And **this** was what he was getting? The disgusting million year old aftershave? **This** was his dad's idea of making up? Unbe-flipping-lievable!

"It's Beast **Pour Homme**," said Brian helpfully, just in case Norm hadn't already worked that out for himself.

"You might not need it at the moment, Norman. But you will **one** day. And if it brings you half as much luck as it brought **me**, you'll be one happy guy."

Norm watched in horror as his parents looked at each other, before actually blowing each other a

272

kiss. Revolting didn't even *begin* to describe it.

"Here, take it," said Norm's dad holding out the bottle towards Norm. "It's yours."

Norm took it.

"Well, love?" said his mum. "Aren't you going to say something?"

"Can I go now?" said Norm.

"Pardon?" said his mum.

"Can I go now, please?"

"Erm, yes," said Norm's mum. "If you want."

"It's fine," said Norm's dad as Norm got up out of the armchair. "I think he's a little bit overwhelmed."

Overwhelmed? thought Norm heading for the door. That was **one** way of flipping putting it.

Look out for Norm's NINTH hilarious adventure

THE WORLD OF NORM

MAY STILL BE CHARGED

Coming soon!

Have you read the first hilarious Norm book?

Read on for the first chapter…

Norm knew it was going to be one of those days when he woke up and found himself about to pee in his dad's wardrobe.

"Whoa! Stop Norman!" yelled Norm's dad, sitting bolt upright and switching on his bedside light.

UH? UH?

UH?

"Uh? What?" mumbled Norm, his voice still thick with sleep.

"What do you think you're doing?"

"Having a pee?" said Norm, like this was the most stupid question in the entire history of stupid questions.

"Not in my wardrobe you're not!" said Norm's dad.

"That's from Ikea that is," added Norm's mum, like it was somehow OK to pee in a wardrobe that wasn't.

Norm was confused. The last thing he knew he'd been on the verge of becoming the youngest ever World Mountain Biking Champion, when he'd suddenly had to slam on his brakes to avoid hitting a tree. Now here he was having to slam on a completely different kind of brakes in order to avoid a completely different kind of accident. What was going on? And what were his parents doing sleeping in the bathroom anyway?

"Toilet's moved," said Norm, hopping from one foot to the other, something which at the age of three was considered socially acceptable, but which at the age of nearly thirteen, most definitely wasn't.

"What?" said Norm's dad.

"Toilet's moved," said Norm, a bit louder.

But Norm's dad had heard what Norm said. He just couldn't quite *believe* what Norm had said.

"No, Norman. It's not the *toilet* that's moved! It's *us* that's moved!"

"Forgot," said Norm.

Norm's dad looked at his eldest son. "Are you serious?"

"Yeah," said Norm, like this was the *second* most stupid question in the entire history of stupid questions.

"You *forgot* we moved house?"

DUH!

"Yeah," said Norm.

"How can you *forget* we moved house?" said Norm's dad, increasingly incredulous.

"Just did," shrugged Norm, increasingly close to wetting himself.

"But we moved over three months ago, Norman!" said Norm's dad.

"Three months, two weeks and five days ago, to be precise," said Norm's mum, like she hadn't even had to think about it.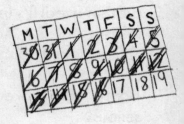

Norm's dad sighed wearily and looked at his watch. It was two o'clock in the morning.

"Look, Norman. You just can't go round peeing in other peoples' wardrobes and that's all there is to it!"

"I didn't," said Norm.

"No, but you were *about* to!"

Norm's dad was right. Norm *had* been about to pee in the wardrobe, but he'd managed to stop himself just in time.

Typical, thought Norm. Being blamed for something he hadn't actually done.

Norm considered arguing the point, but by now his bladder felt like it was the size of a space hopper. If he didn't pee soon he was going to explode. Then he'd *really* be in trouble!

"Go on. Clear off," said Norm's dad.

Norm didn't need telling twice and began waddling towards the door like a pregnant penguin.

"Oh, and Norman?"

"Yeah?" said Norm without bothering to stop.

"The toilet's at the end of the corridor. You can't miss it."

Norm didn't reply. He knew that if he didn't get to the toilet in the next ten seconds there was a very good chance that he *would* miss it!

***

Norm tried every trick he knew to get back to sleep. The trouble was, Norm only knew one trick – counting sheep jumping over a gate – and it just wasn't working. For a start he'd made the gate much too high. There was no way a sheep was going to be able to clear it. Not without some kind of springboard or mini trampoline, anyway. In the end there was a big pile-up of sheep, all milling about like…well, sheep, basically. It was *so* annoying. And the more Norm thought about it the less sleepy he got. And the less sleepy Norm got the less chance there was of carrying on the

dream where he'd left off. Was he destined to become World Mountain Biking Champion or not? Norm was desperate to find out.

Norm tried to guess what time it was. The last time he'd looked it had been 2.30. That seemed like ages ago. But it was hard to tell. It was still pitch black outside. A couple of cars had driven up and down the street and some random guy had wandered past, singing tunelessly at the top of his voice. Norm opened one eye to check. The red digits of the digital clock glowed, suspended in the dark.

2:33ᴀᴍ

Norm couldn't believe it. Three minutes? Was that *really* all it had been since he'd last looked? Three measly minutes? A hundred and eighty stupid seconds? A twentieth of a flipping hour? No way, thought Norm. That can't be right. The clock must be faulty. The battery must have run out. The world must have stopped turning. There *had* to be a rational explanation. It couldn't possibly have been only *three* minutes! But it was. He was never *ever* going to get back to sleep at this rate!

It didn't help that Norm could hear his dad, snoring away like a constipated rhinoceros. Not that Norm had ever actually heard a constipated rhinoceros – but he imagined that's what one would have sounded like. He'd never noticed how loud it was before. Before they'd moved house, that is. Their old house had been solid and sound proof. There could literally have *been* a constipated rhinoceros in their old house and Norm wouldn't have heard it. But in this house, with its tiny rooms and paper-thin walls, you could virtually hear fingernails growing.

Norm tried putting his pillow over his head but it didn't make the slightest bit of difference. It was an incredible racket. It wouldn't have been so bad,

but his mum and dad's room wasn't even next to Norm's! How come his mum could sleep through it and yet Norm couldn't? How come his stupid little brothers could sleep through it and yet Norm couldn't? It was just so unfair, thought Norm. But then so was everything these days.

Like being blamed for peeing in his dad's wardrobe for instance. Or rather, *not* peeing in his dad's wardrobe. How unfair was that? It wasn't Norm's fault they'd moved was it? It would never have happened in their old house. In their old house he'd never once woken up to find himself about to pee in anything *other* than a toilet. In their old house Norm would have been back to sleep ages ago!

The more Norm thought about it, the more wound up he got. Why on earth did they have to go and move in the first place? Who in their right minds would leave a nice big house for a glorified rabbit hutch? Well, not exactly big. It wasn't like it was massive or anything. But compared to this place their old house was like Buckingham flipping Palace!

By now, Norm was oozing anger. The air around him practically crackled, as if he was some kind of human electricity generator. Never mind flipping wind-farms or solar flipping panels. If harnessed correctly, Norm could have single-handedly powered a small town for a whole year!

It was probably just as well then that Norm *didn't* hear Brian, his middle brother, pad along the landing and open his parents' bedroom door. It was probably just as well that he *wasn't* there to see Brian lift the lid of the laundry basket and pee in it. And it was *definitely* just as well that Norm *didn't* see Brian pad away again without so much as a peep from his parents, one of whom was still snoring like a constipated rhinoceros and the other of whom was busy dreaming of her next trip to IKEA.

A car drove down the street, the beam of its headlights flickering through a crack in the curtains and briefly illuminating Norm's face. But amazingly, Norm never even noticed. Like a hurricane that had finally blown itself out, Norm had fallen fast and furiously asleep.

The *good* news as far as Norm was concerned was that he picked up the dream exactly where he'd left off. The *bad* news was that his best friend Mikey became the youngest ever World Mountain Biking Champion. Norm came second. It was so unfair.